MW00583476

The Good King

The Good King

BY Brian Boisen

RESOURCE *Publications* • Eugene, Oregon

THE GOOD KING

Resource Publications
An Imprint of Wipf and Stock Publishers
199 W. 8th Ave., Suite 3
Eugene, OR 97401

www.wipfandstock.com

PAPERBACK ISBN: 978-1-6667-8541-8
HARDCOVER ISBN: 978-1-6667-8542-5
EBOOK ISBN: 978-1-6667-8543-2

VERSION NUMBER 08/31/23

for you four

.

Prologue

~

Once upon a time there was a King who was the King of everything. He was the King of everything in the north, and he was the King of everything in the south; he was the King of everything in the east, and he was the King of everything in the west. He was the King of all that was above and all that was below and all that was all around. The King was the King of everyone and everything ever.

— BOOK ONE —
The Good King

Part I

~

The King of everything was a good King. He was a good King because he loved his people. He knew everyone in his Kingdom by name, and his greatest joy was to be with his people, sharing in their lives and bringing them joy. The King of everything loved his people, and his people loved him.

Chapter 1

❧

L ittle Mitzi McDougal was home sick in bed. She had a stuffy nose, a scratchy throat, and a cough deep down in her chest. Her mother had spent all day fluffing her pillows, brewing her tea, and serving her soup. By evening, she was exhausted.

Just after supper, there was a knock on the door. Mrs. McDougal opened it, and there stood the King. On his face was a kind smile and in his arms was a basket full of odds and ends.

"Good evening, Mary," he said. "I understand your little Mitzi has had a disappointing day."

"Yes, indeed, she has," the girl's mother said, "for today is Mitzi's birthday, but she has been so miserable with her cold we have not been able to celebrate."

"That is very sad," said the King, shaking his head. "I know you have worked very hard caring for your child today, so I have come to give you a little relief and see what I can do to bring Mitzi cheer."

"Thank you, my King," she said. "That is very good of you."

"Think nothing of it," he said, and she led him to little Mitzi's room.

"Hello, Mitzi," said the King, sitting in a chair by the girl's bed.

"Hello, my King," said Mitzi, wiping her nose with a handkerchief and sitting up taller against her pillows. "Thank you for visiting me."

"It is my pleasure," said the King. "I knew it was your birthday, and when I heard about your terrible cold, I came right over. Look what I have brought you."

The King reached into his basket and pulled out a trio of balloons: one red, one blue, and one yellow, and each was held by a silver ribbon as it floated in the air. Mitzi laughed and clapped as she received the balloons. Then the King brought out a covered dish, and when he lifted the lid, he revealed tiny frosted cakes. Mitzi and the King ate three each. Next, the King produced an earthen jug with a cork stopper and two earthen cups. He poured out hot spiced cider, and he and Mitzi drank it down and sighed contentedly.

"Thank you, King," said Mitzi. "That was delicious!"

"You are most welcome, Mitzi," the King said.

He reached into the basket once again. He handed Mitzi a small box wrapped in purple paper, a big box wrapped in green paper, and a medium box wrapped in orange paper, and each box was bound with a golden ribbon tied in a bow. Mitzi unwrapped the small box and found it was filled with chocolates. Next she opened the big box and discovered a pretty woolen coat lined with fur to keep her warm in the winter wind. Then she tore the paper off the medium box and drew out a stuffed brown bear with fuzzy ears, a soft tummy, and kind, amber eyes. Mitzi hugged the little bear tightly.

"Thank you, King," said Mitzi. "These are darling!"

"You are most welcome, Mitzi," the King said.

He brought out a long box from the bottom of the basket, and when he opened its lid, Mitzi saw it was her favorite game. He placed the playing board on top of the covers, and they took turns rolling the dice, moving the figures, and drawing cards until Mitzi won the match by three points. The King laughed and laughed, and he patted Mitzi on the back when her laughter turned into a cough.

"Thank you, King," said Mitzi. "That was delightful!"

"You are most welcome, Mitzi," the King said as he packed the game, bottle, cups, and dish back into his basket.

When all was tidied up, he drew a small book from out of his pocket. "Now, snuggle into your pillows and blankets," he told her, "for I am going to read to you a wonderful tale and it will make you sleepy. I have very much enjoyed being with you, Mitzi. Thank you for sharing your birthday with me."

"Thank you for turning my sadness into joy, my King," Mitzi said as she made herself warm and cozy.

The King began to read from his book, and Mitzi's thoughts were filled with mountains and castles, brave knights and clever princesses, the cunning of dragons and the virtue of heroes. Soon, she drifted off to sleep.

As they stood at the door, the King said, "I believe Mitzi will have a good night's sleep now, which means you will be able to get some rest as well, Mary."

"Thank you for all your kindness, my King," she said.

"It was a gift to me to be able to celebrate Mitzi's birthday with her," said the King. "She is a precious child. Now I will be off, but I will see you both soon!" He gave Mary a hug and stepped out into the night.

Chapter 2

∼

F armer Xiao was having trouble. It was time to prepare his fields for sowing seeds to produce the year's harvest, but when Xiao placed the yoke upon his oxen, one of them stepped right onto his foot. He found he could not stand or walk, for his foot had been broken and the pain was terrible.

Early the next day, Xiao was hobbling about the farmyard with his leg in a splint, when he looked out and saw the King walking along the lane at the edge of his land. The King smiled and waved.

"Good morning, Song Xiao, my friend!"

"Good morning to you, my King!"

"I understand you are having trouble," said the King as he crossed the yard.

"Yes, indeed, I am. It is time to plow my fields in preparation for planting, but I have broken my foot and cannot manage it. My neighbors are all busy with their own work, and my children live far away. I do not know what I am going to do."

"Then I will help you," said the King. "But I will need you to instruct me, for I am a king and not a farmer."

"Thank you very much, my King," Xiao said. "First we must remove the stones from the fields." He found heavy boots, sturdy britches, and a weathered tunic for the King to wear. Then he guided the King in calling the oxen together, securing the yoke around their necks, and attaching the wagon hitch to the yoke. Xiao hobbled along as the King led the oxen around the fields hunting for scattered stones and hoisting them into the wagon.

When he had gathered them all and unloaded them into a pile beside Xiao's barn, they took a break and had the tea, honey biscuits, and hard-boiled eggs Song Mei had prepared for them. They sat and ate together, talking about the weather, events in the village, and happenings across the Kingdom.

Once they finished their meal, the King said, "Thank you for a wonderful breakfast, Mei. And now, Song Xiao, let us go and continue the day's work."

"Thank you, my King," Xiao said, and he led the King back out to his fields. He instructed the King in how to attach the plow's harness to the yoke and guide the oxen forward to make rows of churned up earth across his fields. Xiao limped along with the King, offering him coaching and encouragement as he plowed.

When they had finished plowing the fields, they took a break and shared the chicken, vegetables, and noodles in a savory broth Song Mei had cooked for them. They sat and ate together, and the couple told the King stories of their lives growing up as children in the same village, of their wedding and of their children, and of all the joys and heartaches they had experienced over the years. The King listened, sharing in their laughter and their tears.

Once they finished their meal, the King said, "Thank you for a delicious lunch, Mei. And now, Song Xiao, let us go and finish the day's work."

"Thank you, my King," Xiao said, and he led the King back out to his fields. He taught the King which seeds to sow, where to sow them, and how each kind of seed was best sown into the soil. Under Xiao's guidance, the King planted rows of cabbages, celery, and spinach, lanes of tomatoes, cucumbers, and squash, aisles of string beans, snow peas, and eggplants, and lines of many other vegetables. Then he sowed acres of corn, wheat, and soybean.

When they had completed planting the seeds, they returned to Xiao's home, washed up, and sat down for the fresh trout, snow peas, and steamed rice Song Mei had made for them. As they ate together, the King told them stories of his life in the palace, of funny things he had seen, and of the struggles and triumphs of his people across his Kingdom. Song Xiao and Mei listened, sharing in his laughter and his tears.

Once they finished their meal, the King said, "Thank you, Mei, for a delicious supper. And now, Song Xiao, it is time for me to go."

Farmer Xiao said, "Thank you, my King, for all your help. I don't know what I would have done without you."

"I am very grateful for my time with you and Mei, and for a chance to learn more about farming," said the King. "Now I know who the hardest workers in my Kingdom are!" He embraced the couple and walked back down the lane.

Chapter 3

∽

The Widow Mukondi sat and stared in her small cottage. She sat and stared in grief and in anger, for her husband had died and her heart was broken in his absence. "Why?" she asked. "Why?" she raged.

Her neighbors tried to comfort her. They spoke gentle words to her. They brought her food to eat and water to drink. They cleaned her house, cared for her goats, and collected eggs from her chickens. The Widow Mukondi neither responded to their words nor thanked them for their troubles. She only sat and stared. "Why?" she asked. "Why?" she raged.

When the sun went down, her neighbors said their good nights and left for their own homes, and the Widow Mukondi sat and stared in the darkness of her small cottage. The King sat across from her.

"I am here with you, Anyango," the King said.

"Why?" she asked. "Why?" she raged. "My husband is dead. Why were you not with him?"

"I was with him, Anyango," the King said. "After you watched over him through the long hours of each day until you could stay awake no longer, I sat and watched with Okeyo through the long hours of each night until you awoke."

The King reached over and touched the wick of a candle, and it sprang to life. The flame flickered and wobbled, illuminating the Widow Mukondi's face with its warm, wavering glow. She sat and stared at the King with her grief and anger.

"I am here with you, Anyango, and I love you," the King said.

"Why?" she asked. "Why?" she raged. "My husband is dead. Why did you not love him?"

"I did love him, Anyango," the King said. "I knew Okeyo since he was a boy, and we spent much time together over the years. We walked together and talked together, and we shared in many good works together. We laughed, sang, and told stories together, and we wondered at the great wide world together. Okeyo was my friend and I loved him dearly."

The King reached over and took the Widow Mukondi's hands into his own. She did not withdraw them, but sat and stared at the King with her grief and anger.

"I am with you, Anyango. I love you, and I share in your grief," the King said.

"Why?" she asked. "Why?" she raged. "My husband is dead, and I do not know what to do with all the grief and all the anger in my heart. I hurt so badly, my King, and I do not know how to live now that Okeyo is gone."

The King took her into his arms and held her, and at last the tears came. The Widow Mukondi and the King wept long together, shaking, sobbing, and wailing in each other's arms. When the tears subsided, they spoke together of Okeyo, of his bright eyes and winsome smile, of his strong arms and skilled hands, and of his good, kind, faithful heart. The Widow Mukondi spoke of how much she missed the sound of his voice, the scent of his skin, and the touch of his hand. She spoke of her worries over how she would live without Okeyo's support and protection. She spoke of her feelings of being lost and alone.

When the Widow Mukondi fell silent, the King said, "Anyango, my precious daughter, I share your grief and understand your worries, but know that you are not alone. I am with you and I love you, and your neighbors are with you and they love you, and together we will work by your side and make sure you are supported and protected. You are grieving, and that is right and good, but you are not lost, for I will never leave you nor forsake you."

The King stood and helped the Widow Mukondi to her feet. He led her over to the table where the various foods her neighbors brought sat in their dishes. The King took two bowls and filled them with rice, and on top of the rice he placed a spoonful of beans, of corn, of potatoes, and of peas, and on top of them he placed a spoonful of spiced lamb. They ate together and spoke together, and as they cleaned up after their meal, they sang together one of Okeyo's favorite songs. At last, the King tucked the Widow Mukondi into bed.

"Rest now, Anyango," the King said. "Your neighbors love you, and they will be back in the morning, and I love you, and I am always with you. Together we will live another day."

"Thank you, my King," she said, and closed her eyes.

The King kissed the Widow Mukondi on her brow, blew out the candle, and was gone.

Part II

$\sim$

The King of everything was a good King. He was a good King because he loved his people, and he honored them above himself. He did not concern himself with the ways his people could serve him, but, instead, he continuously sought better ways to encourage, support, and bless them. Whenever his people were in need, he would take from what was his own and generously share it.

Chapter 1

~

Once, a great famine came upon the Kingdom. The clouds fled, the rains failed, and a dry, hot wind blew as the sun beat down upon the land. The crops began to wither and die, the sheep and cattle grew thin and sickly, and the people cried out to their King.

The King gathered his engineers and said, "Go across the Kingdom and create new wells for my people. Dig them deep beyond the reach of this drought so they may have water for their crops, their livestock, and their own parched lips. Go quickly, for my people are in need." His engineers went and did all the King had said, but still the drought worsened.

The King next called his managers together and said, "Open my silos, fill my wagons, and distribute my grain across the Kingdom. Be generous with my people so they may have enough to feed their herds and preserve their livelihood. Go quickly, for my people are in need." His managers went and did all the King had said, but still the famine spread.

The King then summoned his servants together and said, "Open my pantries, larders, and cellars, and gather every provision I have. Be generous so everyone may eat their fill and be sustained. Go quickly, for my people are in need." The King joined his servants, and they traveled across the Kingdom distributing his meats, vegetables, and bread to all his people.

Everyone struggled, yet they were able to endure the famine. Soon, the rains returned, the drought was over, and the people resumed their lives.

Chapter 2

$\sim$

A nother time, a great flood came upon the Kingdom. Throughout the winter, storms traveled one after another across the land, covering everything with snow and packing the mountains in ice. As spring came, temperatures rose and began melting the ice, and thunderstorms drenched the land with heavy showers. The continuous rainfall combined with the quickening thaw, and rivers overflowed their banks, lakes swelled above their shores, and valleys filled with swirling eddies of muddy waters. As their lives became threatened, the people cried out to their King.

The King summoned his workmen together and said, "Go across the Kingdom and fill sandbags to protect my people's homes and shops. Build levees along the banks of the rivers and construct dams across their tributaries. Do all you can to hold back the great flow and direct the water away from the towns and villages. Go quickly, for my people are in need." His workmen went and did all the King had said, but still the waters rose.

Recognizing the danger, the King then gathered his messengers together and said, "Go across the Kingdom and call my people to abandon their homes and come join me in my palace. Help my people fill carts and wagons with their possessions and lead their animals along the roads. Go quickly, for my people are in need." His messengers went out and did all the King had said, and soon people from across the Kingdom arrived wet and bedraggled at the Royal Palace. Their animals were sheltered in the King's barns, their possessions were stored in the King's warehouses, and the people gathered together in the King's great hall. An enormous fire burned in the hearth, and all the people were given towels and dry clothes, as well as hot chocolate and steaming bowls of stew. At night they slept in warm beds that had been placed in every room throughout the palace, and during the day they gathered back into the great hall to be with the King. They all ate warm food together, and the King led them in singing songs, playing games, and telling tales to pass the time. For many days, the King and his servants cared for his people in the palace.

At last, the storms passed, the rains ceased, and the waters subsided. The people joined the King and his servants in the work of cleaning up after the flood and salvaging what they could. The King then called his loggers together and said, "Go and harvest timber from my forests." And to his sawyers he said, "Go and mill the timber into lumber." And to his carpenters he said, "Go and use the lumber to rebuild the people's houses, shops, and towns."

Soon the work was completed, and the people were able to return to their homes and resume their lives.

Chapter 3

~

Y et another time, a great plague came upon the Kingdom. The
people's heads began to ache, their noses began to run, and
their throats became sore. Sickness spread across the land, and the
people cried out to their King.

The King called his nurses together and said, "Go out across
the Kingdom and care for my people. Enter their homes and brew
tea, toast bread, and cook soup for them. Change their sheets, fluff
their pillows, and pile blankets high upon their beds. Go quickly,
for my people are in need!" His nurses did everything they could to
bring the people nourishment, comfort, and rest, but still the sickness worsened. The people became feverish, coughed from deep in
their chests, and their stomachs cramped and churned.

The King then sent for his physicians, and said, "Go out across
the Kingdom and tend to my people. Put thermometers under their
tongues, cold cloths upon their brows, and listen to their hearts and
lungs. Administer tonics, tinctures, and serums as you see fit. Go
quickly, for my people are in need!" His physicians did everything
they could to alleviate their symptoms and combat their illness,
but the sickness worsened. The people's fevers rose, they gasped for
breath, and blisters burst across their skin.

Finally, the King himself went out across the Kingdom to
save his people. He entered each person's home, laid his hand
upon their brow, and spoke their name. He moved quickly from
village to village and house to house, pouring out his own power
upon each of his beloved subjects, until he came to the last village
and to the last house and to the last person who was infected. He

whispered the little boy's name and laid his shaking hand upon his brow. Then the King collapsed on the floor.

Across the Kingdom, the people's fevers broke, they breathed easier, and their stomachs relaxed. Strength filled their hearts and their limbs, and they rose and worked together to transport the King back to his palace. They tucked him into bed and gave him tea and warm broth. Day after day, they took turns sitting by his side and keeping watch, until, weeks later, the King's strength was restored. He gave instructions to his servants to organize a great banquet, and he celebrated the passing of the plague with all his beloved people.

Part III

~

The King of everything was a good King. He was
a good King because he loved his people and
honored them above himself, and because he ruled
his Kingdom with laws that were just and true. The
King had two laws. The first was, "You shall honor
all others above yourself." The second was, "You shall
honor me above all others." With these two laws the
King was able to maintain peace amongst his people
and strength throughout his Kingdom.

Chapter 1

~

L ittle Fareed was enjoying time with his cousin, Azim. They played hide-and-seek, then they kicked a ball to each other, then they ran as hard as they could to see who was the fastest. When Azim won the race, little Fareed said, "Azim, you have the intelligence of a donkey, and you smell like a camel." Hearing these words, Azim began to cry.

The King came, gathered Azim into his arms, and held him until his sobs subsided. Then he turned to the boy's cousin and asked, "Fareed, did saying Azim has the intelligence of a donkey and smells like a camel honor him above yourself?"

"No, my King," Fareed answered, "it did not honor my cousin at all."

"You have spoken truly, Fareed," said the King. "And knowing how much I love Azim, did saying such things honor me above all others?"

"No, my King," Fareed sniffed, "my words did not honor you." Then Fareed began to cry, and the King gathered him into his arms and held him until his sobs subsided.

When he calmed himself, Fareed stood and went over to his cousin. "Azim, I am very sorry for my hurtful words. You are far more intelligent than a donkey, and you smell nothing like a camel. Would you please forgive me?"

Azim smiled and said, "Yes, Fareed, I forgive you. Thank you for your apology." The cousins hugged each other.

"That is very good," said the King. "I love you, Fareed, and I love you, Azim; and I honor you both above myself. When you dishonor each other, you dishonor me, and when you hurt each other, you hurt my heart as well. Can you both remember that?"

"Yes, my King," Fareed and Azim answered together.

"Good!" said the King. "Now, let us play catch!" He produced a red ball, and they spread out and threw it to each other. The three of them ran, romped, and laughed together throughout the afternoon.

Chapter 2

∼

Andrei Koslov was a tenant farming on Ivan Smirnoff's estate, and his rent was half of each year's crop. Andrei and his family worked hard, and they were able to pay their rent for several years, but there came a season when the yield was poor, and the next was even worse. Though it left the Koslovs impoverished, Ivan Smirnoff insisted his tenants fulfill their obligations.

The Koslov family became hungry, and each member took on whatever extra work they could find. However, Andrei's daughter, Annika, began to sneak out each night and pilfer food from the Smirnoffs. First, she stole a sack full of potatoes, next, she swiped a basket full of onions, then she snatched a bushel full of corn.

When Annika returned to pinch a clutch of hens, the chickens startled and began beating their wings and squawking. A shrill voice shouted, "What is the meaning of this?" Annika turned and saw Ivan Smirnoff's daughter, Irina, standing behind her holding a pitchfork. "Ah!" Irina said. "Just as I thought! The Koslov family are thieves and scoundrels!"

"No!" said Annika. "My family is innocent. And though I may be a thief and a scoundrel, I am these things only because my family is hungry. You and your family are misers and wretches, enjoying your wealth with no thought to your neighbors."

"Easy words to say when you have been caught red-handed," said Irina. "Now, come with me or I will run you through. You must face the law!"

"I am the law," said the King, "and I do not see my laws being fulfilled here by either of you."

"My King, I discovered Annika Koslov in the act of stealing from my family," Irina said. "I demand justice for this crime."

"Justice is my greatest desire," said the King, "and my laws are its greatest source. Tell me, Irina Smirnoff, my beloved daughter, does threatening your neighbor with a pitchfork honor her above yourself?"

"What? Well, no, my King. But . . ."

"And does doing nothing to help meet your neighbors' needs when they are hungry honor them above yourself?"

"No, my King. But . . ."

"And does leaving your neighbors impoverished by requiring the immediate payment of their debts honor them above yourself?"

"No, my King," Irina said.

"And knowing I love Andrei and his family dearly, and that the very land upon which you live and all it produces belongs to me, does any of this honor me above all others?"

"No, my King," Irina said with a tear in her eye. "I understand, and I am grieved that my family and I have neglected your laws and brought sorrow upon our neighbors. Please forgive us."

"Thank you, Irina Smirnoff," the King said. "I do forgive you. I had hoped your family would be my representatives, and, out of the abundance with which I have blessed you, you would help meet the needs of your neighbors. Please keep this in mind in the future."

"Yes, my King," Irina said. "We will."

"Now," said the King, "Annika Koslov, my beloved daughter, do you understand what you have done?"

"Yes, my King," Annika said. "In stealing from my neighbors, I have failed to honor them above myself, and have thus broken your first law."

"Yes," said the King. "And what else?"

"Because you love my neighbors and are the true owner of all they possess, in stealing from them, I have failed to honor you above all others."

"Yes," said the King. "And what else?"

Annika frowned for a moment, then brightened. "Ah! I now see I should have come to you with the needs of my family. You love us and always honor us above yourself; I should have trusted in your love."

"That is good, my daughter," said the King, "but do you think of this only now?"

Annika looked away, then her lip quivered, and a tear ran down her cheek. "No, my King. I knew all along I should come to you, but I acted out of anger and spite. In every way, I have failed to honor you."

"That is true," said the King. "I dearly love Ivan and his family and would not have them stolen from. But, far more, I want you to trust in my love. I will always meet your needs and the needs of your family, if you allow me to."

"I know you are a good and faithful King," Annika said, "and I will try very hard to hold on to your promise and trust in your love." Turning to her neighbor, she said, "Irina Smirnoff, I am so very sorry for my crimes against you and your family. Please forgive me. And please allow me to make reparations for what I have stolen. I will work until the cost has been paid."

"I do forgive you," Irina said. "But now I understand that my family's ungracious actions led to your folly. Please let us help meet your family's needs until you are able to sustain yourselves once again. Along with that, I myself will work by your side until we have earned enough to compensate for the things you stole. Come, my friend, let us make everything right together."

"Very good," said the King. "Now, why don't you both join me in my orchard tomorrow? It is harvest time and we have many apples to pick. Let us work together, and I will pay you handsomely towards the debt that is owed."

With plans in place and his law restored, the King said farewell to his friends.

Chapter 3

~

T he Duke of Westerfield challenged the Earl of Essex to a bat-
tle. The two lords gathered their armies together, marched
them out, and arrayed them across opposite sides of the green.
They placed battalions of foot soldiers in the front, divisions of
cavalry behind them, and companies of archers in the rear. The
two lords positioned themselves atop the high hills on either end
of the battleground.

Once everything was arranged, the Duke of Westerfield
raised a green flag, and the Earl of Essex waved one in return. Each
shouted to his people, "All is ready! Infantry, prepare your charge!
Cavalry, marshal your horses! Archers, nock your arrows!" Everyone did as they were told. Then the two lords yelled, "Ready! Set!
Go!" The infantry began to run, the war horses snorted and reared,
and the archers released a volley of arrows.

Suddenly, the King appeared with his arms outstretched in
the center of the battlefield. "Stop!" he commanded in a mighty
voice that echoed across the plain. The foot soldiers stumbled to a
halt, the mounted steeds froze in place, and the arrows burst into
flames and fell to the ground in ashes. "Westerfield! Essex!" thun-
dered the King. "Come and stand before me!"

The two noblemen descended their high hills, and, wide-eyed
and trembling, they approached the King. Once they stood before
him, each managed to murmur, "Yes, my Lord?"

"What is the meaning of this?" the King demanded. "Why
are these men bearing swords, pikes, and clubs with murder in
their eyes? Why are these horses arrayed with armor and their

riders brandishing spears? Why do these archers aim deadly arrows at their brothers?"

"Ah, yes, my Lord, as to that," began Westerfield, "we have discovered a rather rich vein of pure silver running along the border between our lands. Whichever of us claims the load for himself shall gain considerable wealth. Essex and I decided to put it to a friendly contest of arms, with mining rights as the prize to the victor."

"Yes," said Essex, "we wanted to settle the matter like gentlemen and not make too great a fuss over it. We are both quite wealthy already, of course. We considered it more a matter of sport than of war, if you understand me."

The King's eyes blazed. "Sport?" he asked. "Tell me, Essex, is a silver mine worth the lives of all these men?"

Essex looked nervously at the soldiers standing in formation. "Well, perhaps not all of them."

"And what do you say, Westerfield?" the King beseeched the other man. "Would such wealth be worth ten of their lives?"

"Now that you put it that way," said the Duke, "I suppose ten lives would be too great a price."

"Tell me, either of you," pleaded the King, "would any prize be worth the suffering and death of even one of these men?"

"No, my King," they said, ashamed.

"So, then, by instigating this conflict, are you honoring the lives of your men above your own?" asked the King.

"No," they said.

"No, you are not," said the King. "And be clear: I am the King of everything. These men are my subjects. I know each of them by name, and I love them all dearly. And the vein of silver running along your borders belongs to me. In fact, the very lands you call your own are first and foremost my possessions; I have merely entrusted them to your care. Understanding all this, do your actions today honor me above all others?"

"No, my King," they said.

"I have violated your laws," said Essex, "and I am grieved. Please forgive me, My King."

"As am I," said Westerfield, "and I desire to make reparations, if I may."

"Yes, you may," said the King. "I know both of you and love you dearly, and I desire your greatest good. And what would be best for you and for your people is if you all shared in both mining the silverload and benefiting from its yield together. This is a great gift from me, so distribute the wealth equally between yourselves and amongst your people. Enrich each other's lives by honoring each other above yourselves; and in so doing, you will honor me above all others. Fulfill my laws, and you will be blessed."

The King of everything was a good King. He loved his people, and his people loved him. He knew everyone in his Kingdom by name, and his greatest joy was to be with his people, to share in their lives, and to help them in times of need. He guided them with wisdom, justice, and grace, and everyone prospered.

— BOOK TWO —
The Rebellion

Part I

∾

Within the Kingdom of the King of everything, there was a Merchant. The Merchant traveled across the Kingdom buying and selling goods. He offered the people whatever indulged their fancies, distinguished them above each other, and gave them the advantage in their dealings together. The Merchant would find rare items of beauty, cunning, and power, and he would sell them to whomever met his price.

Chapter 1

~

L ucia Sosa was unhappy. She looked in the mirror and sighed, seeing the reflection of a woman who appeared to be quite plain compared to her neighbor, Martina Cortez. She walked around her house and groaned, knowing that, compared to Martina Cortez's home, her furnishings were modest and her decorations were drab. She looked at her husband, Pablo, and moaned, wishing he could be as handsome and dashing as Martina Cortez's husband, Sergio. Lucia Sosa was very unhappy.

One day there came a knock at Lucia's front door. When she opened it, she was surprised to see the Merchant standing on her porch holding a number of cases. "Who, may I ask, are you?"

"I am a vendor of rare and wonderful goods, my lady," said the Merchant. "May I come in and show you my wares? I feel confident they will be to your liking."

Lucia invited the Merchant in, and he first opened a tall case. "Here is a selection of dresses made of the finest silks from the east," he said. "They have been woven to perfection, dyed in an array of brilliant colors, and cut to accentuate your most alluring features."

"They are quite beautiful!" Lucia cried.

Next, the Merchant opened a medium-sized case. "Here is an assortment of the finest jewelry from the north," he said. "The gold is of the purest quality, the pearls are strung to highlight your curves, and the gems are so dazzling no one will be able to take their eyes off you."

"They are most magnificent!" Lucia exclaimed.

The Merchant then opened a smaller case. "Here is a collection of the finest cosmetics from the west," he said. "The powders are mixtures of the best minerals and ores, the pastes are blends of the purest oils and waxes, and the perfumes are tinctures of the most exotic blossoms and resins. When applied with skill, your eyes will be captivating, your lips inviting, and your scent maddening."

"They are truly ingenious!" Lucia gasped.

"Why don't you slip yourself into one of the dresses, adorn yourself with some of the jewels, fashion for yourself an application of the cosmetics, and see what you think?"

Lucia made her selections and excused herself. When she returned, the Merchant smiled approvingly. The crimson silks clung about her legs, wrapped around her waist, and boosted up her bosom. The jewels sparkled from her ears, around her throat, and on her fingers. The cosmetics glittered and shimmered, creating the face of a young debutante.

The Merchant held up a mirror and asked, "What do you see?"

"I see a woman who is exceptionally exquisite," Lucia purred.

"And what might such a woman be able to achieve for herself?" asked the Merchant.

"Such a woman could walk across the street and knock on Martina Cortez's door. She could show Martina Cortez that she is not the most beautiful woman in the world. She could capture the heart of Martina Cortez's husband, Sergio, and win all his swaggering passion for herself. She could take possession of Martina Cortez's home and everything she owns with all its extravagance. Such a woman could have whatever she desires, and more."

"Do you want to be such a woman?" the Merchant asked.

"Yes, I do," Lucia Sosa said. She paid the Merchant his price.

Chapter 2

~

F riedrich Werner was very happy indeed. His bakery was thriving in every way: his breads and pastries were considered the finest around, he offered the widest variety to be had, and his sales outstripped every other bakery by far. He was praised and honored by all as the premier baker of their city.

One day, the Merchant entered Friedrich's bakery and ordered a cinnamon roll. When he had finished eating, he licked his lips and declared, "That was the best pastry I have ever had the pleasure of tasting! I must speak with the proprietor of this illustrious establishment!"

Seeing that the Merchant was a man of means, the counter girl ran to fetch Friedrich. Soon he appeared and greeted the man who had sung such high praises of his pastry.

"My good sir," said the Merchant, "you are a culinary genius! Your talents should be known by all!"

"Well," said Friedrich, "if it is not too boastful, I can tell you my bakery has received many accolades. We are held in high honor throughout this city."

"I should hope so," said the Merchant. "But being honored in one city is not enough! You should be revered across the Kingdom!"

"The Kingdom!" Friedrich laughed, delighted. "That would be wonderful! But I am afraid we are nowhere near large enough an operation to supply baked goods beyond our borders. We lack the staff, the equipment, and the quantity of ingredients, and I do not have the capital needed to expand our efforts."

"Ah!" said the Merchant, "But have you not heard the adage, 'You must spend money to make money'? I can see in your eyes that while you feel you lack the resources for expansion, you most certainly do not lack the vision or the drive to do it. Perhaps we should talk further, for I am in communication with a number of manufacturers and suppliers who could help increase your productivity, and I am on intimate terms with a certain banker who would credit you the necessary funds."

A smile crept across Friedrich's face. "Yes," he said, "perhaps we should talk further."

The Merchant introduced Friedrich to his friend the banker, and an advance was arranged for expanding the baker's enterprise.

Next, the Merchant negotiated agreements between Friedrich and various suppliers for the purchase of large quantities of ingredients at a greatly reduced price. Though many of these ingredients would be of a lower quality, the Merchant assured the baker that with the use of certain additives, the flavor and texture of his baked goods would remain delectable to the populace.

The Merchant then brought Friedrich into contact with the manufacturers of automated devices that would mix, bake, and package his breads and pastries at a rapid rate. Though this would eliminate the need for many of the skilled artisans who had been his loyal employees for years, the Merchant assured the baker that sacrifices were necessary for reaching a higher level of productivity.

Lastly, the Merchant connected Friedrich with the maker of mechanical wagons that could transport large quantities of his baked goods across vast distances. With such vehicles, the Merchant assured him, he could distribute his breads and pastries throughout the Kingdom and establish himself as the preeminent baker above all the rest.

"Do you wish such prestige for yourself?" the Merchant asked.

"Yes, I do," Friedrich Werner said. He paid the Merchant his price.

Chapter 3

⤫

T he Barony of Bulwick was a modest barony with a modest number of peasants producing a modest yield of beans each year, and there was only one modest town in the center of its land.

Its neighbor to the east, the Barony of Farmingham, had a thriving agricultural enterprise, producing excessive yields of wheat, barley, and corn, which both supported its own people and allowed them to export to many points across the Kingdom. Farmingham had three towns, each larger than Bulwick's one, and they were known for their many festivals throughout the year.

Bulwick's neighbor to the west, the Barony of Brookshire, had a prosperous manufacturing industry, utilizing the power of a great river flowing through its land to run mills, smithies, and factories. It produced many useful goods that were sold in numerous shops throughout the Kingdom. Brookshire had several towns and one true city which had become an important center of trade.

These three baronies comprised Whitmore County, and the Count of Whitmore devotedly followed the laws of the King. He administered his authority with gentleness and integrity, seeking only to coordinate the efforts of all three baronies to benefit each other and produce mutual harmony.

Although life within Whitmore County was good and all his needs were being met, the Baron of Bulwick was dissatisfied. He had grown weary of being the baron of the least significant barony in the county, but he was uncertain how he might improve his situation.

The Merchant rode upon a stallion across the Bulwick Estate. He led three great canvas-covered wagons pulled by teams of draft horses driven by his servants. When they came to the Baron's manor, the Merchant dismounted, handed the reigns of his steed to an attendant, and walked through the front door without introduction or ceremony. "Get your master," he said to the sputtering butler.

The Baron of Bulwick found the Merchant sitting in his chair behind his desk in his study. "What is the meaning of this?" he demanded.

"Sit down, Bulwick," said the Merchant, and the Baron sat. "We do not have time for pleasantries. Your situation here is abominable."

"What do you mean?" asked the Baron.

"Please," said the Merchant. "I have just toured your neighbors' lands, and they make yours look like the practical joke of a piebald jester."

"Yes," said Bulwick, looking down shamefacedly, "it is true."

"It is inexcusable that such prosperity should be in the hands of men like the Baron of Farmingham and the Baron of Brookshire. You are far and above their superior."

"Oh!" said Bulwick, looking up. "Do you think so?"

"Absolutely!" declared the Merchant. "On top of that, I have spoken with Count Whitmore, and, I have to tell you, he does not have half your ability. He lacks your imagination and ambition, and he has left this county anemic and enfeebled."

"Ah!" said Bulwick, beginning to smile. "That has always been my opinion, but I didn't think it was my place to . . ."

"Your modesty does you credit," the Merchant interrupted, "but the time for decorum is over. You must take action! The moment has come for you to seize control of the county and save it from such ineptitude!"

"This is exciting, I must say," said the Baron, beaming. Then his face fell. "But how?"

"Follow me," commanded the Merchant, and he led the Baron out to where his three wagons were parked along the drive. "Before you stands the way to greatness. Shall I show you?"

"Yes," Bulwick said, his eyes filled with wonder.

"Let us be frank," said the Merchant. "Your ambitions demand nothing short of war, and if you fight a war, you must fight to win. Now, to win a war, you must first be able to approach your enemy without inhibition." The Merchant gestured to the servants standing around the lead wagon. Each pulled a rope and the canvas covering its frame fell away. Sitting atop the bed was what appeared to be another wagon made of iron, with metal plates riveted together to form a great box. The bulky structure rested upon two wide ribbons of tread running around a series of wheels on either side, and on top of the structure stood an armored turret with narrow slits around its circumference. "It is completely impervious to swords, spears, and arrows, and is capable of enduring a direct hit from a catapult," said the Merchant. "It can carry twenty men, and it is self-mobilized, being powered by steam."

"It is truly amazing!" Bulwick said.

"Indeed," said the Merchant. "I am able to obtain as many of these vehicles as you desire. Now, along with the need to approach your enemy, you must be able to inflict great harm upon him once you have arrived." He motioned to the servants standing around the middle wagon, and removing the canvas, they exposed stacks of wooden boxes. The Merchant nodded, and one of his servants opened a crate and pulled out an odd-looking contraption. It was long and black, with a thin tube at one end and a complex array of mechanical devices on the other. "I present to you a new kind of weapon," the Merchant said and winked at the servant. He pointed the device at a marble statue standing in the center of the Baron's lawn, pulled a little lever with his finger, and a series of deafening explosions erupted. Bulwick threw himself onto the ground and covered his ears. When the echoes of the blast subsided, the Merchant helped the Baron to his feet. They looked and saw that where the statue had stood there were only fragments of white stone scattered across the turf. "The weapon fires small pieces of lead at a rapid rate, and they pierce wood, stone, and steel, as well as flesh and bone."

"It is truly frightening!" Bulwick said.

"Indeed," said the Merchant. "I am able to arrange for a near limitless supply of these weapons to be made available for you. Now, to assure victory in war, you must not only be able to vanquish the enemies who stand before you, you must also be able to decimate those at a distance." He waved to the servants standing around the last wagon, and they each pulled a rope. What was unveiled baffled the Baron. Laid out across the flatbed was a long, wide metal tube with a sharp cone on one end and fins on the other.

"It looks like a very large arrow," he said.

"Indeed, it does," said the Merchant, "and, in many ways, that is exactly what it is. But this is a very large arrow that is propelled through the air by its own engine, and it is able to cover vast distances at great speeds towards a precisely calculated target. And, once it hits its bullseye, it creates an explosion of unimaginable force leaving behind absolute devastation. You only need two such devices: one to use as a demonstration, and the other to hold as a threat."

"It is truly terrifying," said Baron Bulwick, eyes gleaming. "I love it! With such weaponry, I would be able to take command of the whole county. I could become the Count!"

"Yes," said the Merchant. "But the County of Whitmore is just the beginning. I see an earldom in your future! Nay, a dukedom! Dare I say . . . a kingdom? Do you, Baron Bulwick, desire such glory?"

"Yes, I do," Bulwick said. He paid the Merchant his price.

Part II

~

As the people purchased for themselves more and more items of beauty, cunning, and power from the Merchant, they began to question the goodness of the King and the wisdom of his laws. A great disturbance began to spread across the Kingdom.

Chapter 1

~

T he King's people grew discontented, and they no longer wanted to honor all others above themselves.

~

Lotta Lundgren chewed on a piece of chocolate. It was extra
chewy, for it had caramel in its center. Lotta had purchased many
chocolates from the Merchant: some with almonds, some with
nougat, and some with toffee. Lotta had many different chocolates,
and she was sampling them all.

Elsa Olsson asked, "Lotta, may I have a taste of one of your
chocolates?"

"No!" said Lotta through a mouth smeared and sticky. "I
bought all these chocolates with my own money and they belong
to me!"

Alva Svensson asked, "Lotta, may I have a taste of one
of your chocolates? Remember how I gave you a taste of my
marzipan-fruity?"

"No!" said Lotta as her tummy gurgled. "My chocolates are
far more delicious than your marzipan-fruity!"

The King said, "Lotta, that is too much candy for you to eat.
Won't you share with your friends?"

"No!" said Lotta with reddened cheeks and squinting eyes.

"But, Lotta," said the King, "Are you honoring Elsa and Alva
above yourself?"

"No, I am not," said Lotta, "but I don't care. I want all the chocolates for myself!"

～

Kamal Mahajan paid for a room at the Lemon Tree Hotel. He quickly unpacked the items he purchased from the Merchant, setting scented candles upon the tables, spreading silk sheets upon the bed, and spraying cologne upon himself.

Soon there was a gentle knock on the door, and Kamal led Adhira Bakshi into the room. They kissed, and Adhira removed her long coat to reveal the laced undergarments she purchased from the Merchant.

There was another knock, and the King stood in the doorway. "What are you two doing?" asked the King. "Kamal, is meeting with Adhira like this honoring Nira, your wife, above yourself? And Adhira, is kissing Kamal honoring Bhajan, your husband?"

"No, it is not," said Kamal, "but I do not care. Adhira is far more beautiful than Nira."

"I do not care, either," said Adhira. "Meeting with Kamal here is far more exciting than my life at home with Bhajan."

～

Aurelio Marcelo purchased a dozen more head of cattle from the Merchant. Unfortunately, Aurelio's fields were not large enough for the extra animals, so he knocked down a portion of Balduino Forte's fence and led his new herd across to graze upon his neighbor's grasses. When Balduino discovered this, he marched over to Aurelio's house and confronted him. The two raised their voices, and Aurelio struck Balduino. Balduino struck back, knocking Aurelio to the ground, and he continued hitting him again and again.

"Stop!" said the King. "Aurelio, what have you done? Is grazing your cattle on Balduino's land honoring him above yourself? And Balduino, is beating Aurelio with your fists honoring him above yourself?"

"No, it is not," said Aurelio, "but I don't care. I need to graze my new cattle somewhere, and Balduino's fields are the closest."

"I don't care, either," said Balduino. "Aurelio has offended me, and I will exact my revenge upon him."

Chapter 2

~

T he King's people grew even more discontented, and they no
longer wanted to honor the King above all others.

~

The Merchant demonstrated a new kind of saw to Gustave Du-
bois that could cut down trees five times faster than any other. He
purchased this saw and proceeded to cut down all the trees filling
his own land and sold the timber to Laurent's Lumber Mill. Laurent
offered to purchase more timber from him, so Gustave cut down all
the trees covering the hills and mountains surrounding his land and
brought the logs to the mill. Laurent told Gustave he would purchase even more timber from him, and so he traveled to the Royal
Preserve and cut down all the trees in the King's forest.

The King came and said, "Gustave, my friend, what have you
done?"

Gustave said, "I purchased an amazing saw from the Merchant and cut down all the trees filling my land, then I cut down
all the trees covering the surrounding hills and mountains, and I
sold the timber to Laurent's Lumber Mill."

"Yes," said the King, "and what else did you do?"

Gustave said, "I cut down all the trees in the Royal Preserve,
and I sold the timber to Laurent as well."

"I am the King of everything," said the King. "This means
you belong to me, Gustave, along with the land you possess,
the hills and mountains surrounding you, and all the trees that

covered them. And, as you certainly knew, this meant the trees of the Royal Preserve belonged to me as well, and that I had put them under my protection. Did cutting down all those trees without my permission honor me above yourself?"

"No, it did not," Gustave admitted, "but I don't care. Harvesting those trees made me a great deal of money, and I would like to make still more."

$\sim$

The Merchant presented machines of various kinds to the industrialists of Pha-Nang City. They purchased mighty excavators and began to dredge the Royal River in search of useful minerals and ores. They acquired giant furnaces and erected forges upon the banks of the Royal River for smelting steel. They procured great cast-molds, tools, and conveyor belts, and still further up the Royal River they built factories for manufacturing all sorts of goods.

All the dredging, smelting, and manufacturing produced great quantities of grit, ash, and wasted chemicals of every kind. They were dumped into the Royal River, and they floated down past the Royal Palace and the farms and villages below, polluting everything along the way.

The King came to the industrialists of Pha-Nang City and asked them, "What are you doing, my people?"

The President of the Dinh-Hao Dredging Company said, "We are dredging, smelting, and manufacturing along the Royal River."

The King asked, "Whose river is the Royal River?"

The President of the Sinh-Bao Steel Works Company said, "It is your river."

The King said, "Yes, and your activities have mutilated and polluted my river, which has caused the death of my fish, the corruption of my crops, and great illness among my people. I am the King of everything, and you, along with everything you have destroyed through your industry, belong to me. Has any of this honored me above yourselves?"

"No, it has not," said the President of the Minh-Tao Manufacturing Company, "but we do not care. Through our ingenuity and hard work, we have brought great prosperity to our shareholders, and we would like to bring even more."

⁓

The Merchant spoke with the King's butler about the value of particular goods in the Royal Palace. The Merchant assured him such goods were quite valuable, and he would be happy to facilitate their sale to certain clientele.

The King's butler spoke with the King's chef, and the chef went to the King's stores and packed away the most delicious of the King's wines, meats, and pastries into baskets.

The King's butler spoke with the King's valet, and the valet went to the King's quarters and hid away the most precious of the King's garments, jewels, and books into boxes.

The King's butler spoke with the King's housekeeper, and the housekeeper went throughout the Royal Palace and stacked away the most elegant of the King's ornaments, artwork, and furnishings into crates.

The King's butler gathered all the baskets, boxes, and crates and loaded them onto the Merchant's wagon. He received sacks of gold in return for the haul.

The King came to his palace and called his staff together. "What have you done, my servants?" he asked.

"We gathered up some odds and ends," said the housekeeper, "and we sold them to the Merchant."

"Why did you do this?" asked the King

"To make extra gold for ourselves," said the valet, "so we could join in the trade happening across the Kingdom and become rich."

"But to whom did those things belong?" asked the King.

"They belonged to you, my King," said the chef.

"Yes," said the King, "the wines, the meats, and the pastries belonged to me. The garments, the jewels, and the books belonged to me. The ornaments, the artwork, and the furniture belonged to me as well. I am the King of everything, and you yourselves belong to me. Did taking and selling all these things honor me above yourselves?"

"No, it did not," said the butler, "but we don't care. We want riches, pleasures, and honors for ourselves like everyone else, and we intend to pursue far more."

Chapter 3

$\sim$

T he people's discontentment set their hearts against the King and his rule. United in their defiance, they all marched together towards the Royal Palace.

Dukes, earls, and barons led their regiments. Their soldiers carried shields and brandished swords, their cavalry officers rode steeds and leveled spears, and their archers strung bows and nocked arrows as they advanced.

Industrialists, tradesmen, and shopkeepers led their employees. Their clerks waved handguns and daggers, their craftsmen wielded chisels and saws, and their laborers hefted hammers and hooks as they strutted onward.

Farmers came with pitchforks and scythes, woodsmen swung axes and mauls, and housewives held butcher knives and skillets at the ready. Even the children advanced with sticks and stones clenched in their tiny fists.

All the people of the Kingdom gathered and surrounded the Royal Palace. A great clamor broke out as they clashed their weapons, stomped their feet, and raised their voices. There were shouts for "Justice!" and cries of "Oppression!" and an overwhelming call for "Freedom!"

"My people."

Despite their uproar, each person heard the voice of the King when he spoke. They turned and saw him positioned atop a high hill sitting tall upon a snowy white charger. He was armored in plate of the finest steel and mail of the purest silver. In his hand was a mighty sword, and on his head was a simple golden crown.

"My people," the King said, "why have you gathered thus against me, brandishing weapons and demanding justice? Have I not given you justice? Have I not honored you above myself? Did I not walk with you, talk with you, and break bread with you? Do I not know each of you by name?

"But now you have assembled yourselves here and are demanding freedom. What would you have freedom from? From me? From my laws? I have called every one of you to look to me, recognizing my authority as the King of everything and embracing the great value I have given to everyone and everything over which I rule. I have called you to love me and to love each other, and we have known peace and prosperity as we lived out this great love together. Is this what you desire freedom from?

"In truth, you have not mustered your forces today because of injustice, but because of the selfishness in your hearts. You believe you will have greater pleasure, prosperity, and power for yourselves if you are rid of my rule, but I tell you this today: as you give free reign to your selfishness, it is you who will bring great injustice against each other. Instead of freedom, you will create nothing but bondage and misery. Remember that I warned you of this."

The King looked out one last time at his people. He saw the faces of the men, women, and children he knew and loved twisted with hatred against him.

"Behold your King!" he shouted as he raised his arm, and his mighty sword burst into flames. Suddenly, there appeared myriads upon myriads of fell warriors made of living light too brilliant to look upon. Burning with a blinding rage, they filled the sky and encircled the people of the Kingdom, clashing their weapons and roaring with fearsome voices. Thunder pealed and lightning flashed across the heavens, and a rushing wind blasted through the crowds. The people screamed and wailed, falling to the ground in terror.

Then, just as suddenly, all was silent and still. The people slowly rose, trembling and looking frantically in every direction. They saw the King standing alone upon the hill dressed in a simple robe of homespun, his arms outstretched.

"I know you, and I love you, and I honor you above myself," he said, tears in his eyes. "How could I bear to bring destruction down upon you?"

The whole assembly stood swaying with wonder as they looked upon their King. Then someone shouted, "Justice!" and another cried, "Oppression!" and several more called out, "Freedom!" Someone screamed, "Death to the King!" and in a moment, every voice in the Kingdom demanded, "Death!"

All at once they were in motion, rushing towards the King. Dukes, earls, and barons led their soldiers, cavalry, and archers across the field. Industrialists, tradesmen, and shopkeepers conducted their clerks, craftsmen, and workers up the hill. Farmers, woodsmen, housewives, and even the children scrambled to its top. Weapons raised, the whole assembly converged upon the King, and, with a great shout, they all began to shoot, hack, beat, and stab, until every bullet was spent, every blade was dulled, every rock was thrown, and every hand was stained with blood.

When they had finished, the crowd staggered back. At their center, where the King had stood, they saw the ground trampled, chopped, and muddy with gore. Nothing else remained.

Part III

~

The people raised their hands in rebellion against their King, and when it was over, the King of everything was gone. There was no Kingdom, for they no longer had a king.

Chapter 1

～

Without the King, the people found themselves unconstrained by his laws. They began to explore their new freedoms.

～

Bahram Rahbar sat at his table eating supper with his family. He tasted his food and frowned. "Kasra, my wife, there is quite a bit of pepper on these lentils."

"Yes," Kasra said, "I like pepper."

"But you know it upsets my stomach," said Bahram.

"Yes," Kasra said, "But I am free, and I like pepper."

Bahram frowned, then he looked at his son. "Bazra, do you have much homework to do this night?"

"Yes," Bazra said. "I have a worksheet to do for mathematics, an essay to write for language skills, and ten items to memorize for science."

"I would be glad to help you, if you'd like," said Bahram.

"Thank you, but I will not need your help," said Bazra. "I am free, and I choose not to do my homework."

Bahram frowned, then he looked across the room and saw many toys, books, and pieces of clothing lying about. He turned to his daughter and said, "Minu, my love, after supper you must gather your things from around the house."

"No," said Minu, "for I am free, and I would much rather run around outside than clean up inside."

Bahram sighed and took another bite of his peppery lentils.

∾

Jakub Kowalski cut chops from a rack of lamb, and, as he wrapped them in butcher paper, he threw in a handful of goat ribs. *I am free,* he thought, *so I am free to seek my own advantage.*

Jakub weighed the package and then placed it on the counter. "One pound of the finest lamb chops," he said. "That will be three silver coins."

Szymon Wozniak reached into one pocket and drew out two silver coins, and from another he selected one coin made of highly polished nickel. *I am free,* he thought, *so I am free to seek my own advantage.*

"Here you are," Szymon said, smiling. "Three silver coins."

"Enjoy your chops," Jakub said, smiling in return.

∾

Mbwana Khoza looked at the many stones filling his field, then he looked up at the hot sun shining down upon him. He sighed, lifted a stone, and placed it into his cart. As he stooped to grab another, he saw Jaali Masuku walking by.

"Good day to you, Mbwana," Jaali said.

"Good day to you, Jaali," said Mbwana. "Come and load these stones into my cart."

"No thank you, Mbwana," Jaali said, "for I am free, and I do not wish to do your work for you."

"I am free as well," said Mbwana, "and I am stronger than you. I will use my freedom to beat you if you do not load these stones into my cart."

"Oh dear," said Jaali, and he began to load the stones into Mbwana's cart. Soon Tambo Lubega came walking by.

"Good day to you, Jaali," Tambo said.

"Good day to you, Tambo," said Jaali. "Come and load these stones into Mbwana's cart."

"No, thank you, Jaali," Tambo said, "for I am free, and I do not wish to do either your work or Mbwana's."

"I am free as well," said Jaali, "and I am stronger than you. I will use my freedom to beat you if you do not load these stones into Mbwana's cart."

"Oh dear," said Tambo, and he began to load the stones into Mbwana's cart.

Chapter 2

~

A s the people explored their freedoms, their life together began
to change.

~

The villagers of Llallani desired wealth, so they applied themselves to the production of jewelry. Their men scoured the creek
beds and mined the hillsides in search of precious stones, their
women crafted all they found into gems, beads, and pendants, and
their children fitted them into necklaces, bracelets, and earrings to
sell at the market. Those who were lame, blind, or weak and unable
to work were pushed aside, and their needs were neglected.

~

The elders of Gunyang desired prosperity, so they consolidated
their wealth and purchased machines to weave cloth, cut patterns,
and sew garments. They hired the men of the town to run their
looms, and the women to operate their presses, and the children to
run the cloth through their sewing machines. The air of the factories became hot, dusty, and foul, and the people became ill as they
worked. The elders carefully monitored their progress, and they
docked their meager wages for any lapse of production.

~

The administrators of Rotterhem County desired abundance, so they expanded the operations of their municipal farms. They hired all the laborers they could find, but when they needed more, they sent companies of their militia out into the surrounding counties and their soldiers captured men, women, and children and brought them back to the city. During the night, they housed them in hastily assembled barracks, and during the day, they put them to work in Rotterhem's fields. Whenever their work slackened, their overseers shouted at them, slapped them, and lashed their backs with whips.

Chapter 3

❧

A s the people exercised their freedoms together, many pursued positions of power. In some regions, the nobility engaged in battles for dominion. In others, industrialists applied their wealth to gain control. In still others, charismatic figures campaigned in elections. Soon the old Kingdom was divided into separate nations.

❧

The leaders of the nations busied themselves with the inner workings of their governments. They issued policies and laws for their people, then they appointed directors to carry out their policies and commissioned officers to enforce their laws. They did everything they could to establish public order and maintain control over their nations. In the midst of it all, prominent citizens exploited the policies and turned them to their advantage, while the commoners felt ever more constricted by the laws that bound them.

❧

The leaders of the nations also occupied themselves with the mechanics of their commerce. They organized their men and women and assigned tasks to each. They co-opted industries and enterprises and directed their activities. They established trade routes and agreements with other nations for importing and exporting goods. They did everything they could to maximize the productivity and increase the prosperity of their nations. In the midst of it all, the rich found opportunities to gain ever more wealth, while the poor spiraled into ever-deepening poverty.

The leaders of the nations also focused their efforts on the promotion of their militaries. They manufactured weaponry, conscripted soldiers, and stockpiled armaments. Stronger nations conquered their weaker neighbors and extended their borders. Larger nations made pacts together, while smaller nations formed alliances in attempts to protect themselves. War, with its death and destruction, became the norm. In the midst of it all, the elite gained ever expanding power, while the civilians were crushed under the weight of powerlessness and fear.

The old Kingdom had passed away, and new nations emerged. The people continued to exercise their freedoms and pursue their agendas, and more and more they experienced the consequences of their rebellion against the King.

— BOOK THREE —
The Restoration

Part I

~

As nations grew, conflicts rose, and suffering spread, many people began to regret their rebellion against the King. They longed for the life they had known with him.

Chapter 1

~

Little Mishka sat quietly on the old stump behind his house. Tears streamed down his cheeks as his parents' shouts echoed across the yard.

"It sounds pretty rough in there," said the King, sitting beside him.

"Yes," Mishka said, wiping his face with the back of his sleeve. "They keep yelling about their freedoms, what one wants and how the other doesn't care. They never seem happy, and they never think of me."

"I am sorry," said the King.

"It wouldn't be so bad," Mishka said, picking up a rock and flinging it at a tin can, "but my friends are all the same. They only want to play the games they want to play, but nobody wants to play the same game at the same time, so we all yell at each other and then go our separate ways. I mostly just sit here alone on this stump."

"I am sorry," the King said again.

"Yeah," Mishka said, trying to grab a cat as it walked by. "We shouldn't have gotten mad at you," he sighed. "Things were pretty good when you were the King. I miss it."

"I miss it, too," said the King.

"Hey," Mishka said, looking up at him, "you could be my King again!"

"I am the King of everything," the King said, "and I always will be. That means I am already your King, Mishka."

"Oh," said Mishka. "Well, that's good. You will be my King, and I will be your Mishka, and I will love you like before."

"I would like that," said the King.

Mishka held a blade of grass between his thumbs. He blew on it, and it made a squeaky noise.

The King blew against the blade of grass he held between his thumbs. It also made a squeaky noise.

"My King," Mishka said, looking up at him.

"Yes, Mishka?" asked the King.

"I'm sorry I threw that rock at you," he said, and more tears trickled down his cheeks.

"Thank you," said the King. "I love you, Mishka, and I forgive you."

"Thank you," Mishka said, taking the King's hand and holding it in his own. "I love you, too. I am glad you are my King."

The King gave his hand a squeeze and said, "I am glad you are my Mishka."

They heard the angry voices of Mishka's parents growing louder within the house.

"I did not wish to hurt any of my people when they wanted to take my Kingdom from me," the King said. "But now they are hurting each other and themselves. It is time for me to pull my Kingdom back together again."

"That would be good," Mishka said, poking a stick into the dirt. "Maybe I can help you?"

"I would like your help, Mishka," the King said, patting the boy on his shoulder. "It will be a lot of work, though. Are you up for it?"

"If I can be with you, then I'm up for anything," Mishka said, patting the King on his arm.

"Then let us begin," said the King. He stood, and Mishka stood by his side.

Chapter 2

~

They gathered around an assortment of tables and chairs assembled in Rodrigo and Martina Torres' living room. Tomas Hernandez and Felipe Medina spoke together of weather forecasts for the summer. Maria Ruiz and Elena Delgado discussed the quality of the eggs their chickens had been producing. Olivia Gonzalez chased her little Diego around the room in an attempt to wrangle him into a highchair. Young Vanessa Torres and Juliana Sanchez whispered together, and they giggled as they watched young Pablo Hernandez stand awkwardly in the corner of the room.

Martina came out of the kitchen carrying baskets of towel-wrapped tortillas. Rodrigo followed her, hefting a steaming pot of carnitas smothered in onions and peppers. They added them to the other items already set along the counter. "Time to eat!" Rodrigo announced.

Everyone took turns piling food on their dishes and finding seats at the tables. They immediately commenced with eating, and the room was filled with the sounds of clinking, scraping, and chewing.

"Who made these tamales?" Felipe asked. "They are perfect!"

Tomas smiled. "That would be my Daniela."

"The chile relleno is delicious, Maria, as always," Alonso Navarro said.

"Now you know why I am so fat," Joaquin laughed. "Your daughter spoils me!"

"I am going to have to have a second helping of your carnitas, Rodrigo," said the King. "They are as good as ever."

"Thank you, my King," Rodrigo said. "It is an honor to have you in my home again."

"Yes," Elena said, "It is a blessing to be with you." Everyone agreed.

"I am glad," said the King. "Thank you all for gathering together to share this meal with me. As always, it is my greatest joy to be with you."

A thoughtful silence fell upon the gathering, except for the soft sound of little Diego squeezing frijoles in his pudgy fists. Then Rodrigo stood up. "I am so sorry, my King, for raising arms against you. It was petty, foolish, and vile of me. I had become so selfish and I resented your claims on me. I now see the error of my ways, and I beg your forgiveness."

Maria stood. "I am so sorry, my King, for defying you the way I did. I had become consumed with greed, and I knew you would not approve of my schemes. My ambitions have only led to regret, and I want nothing more to do with them. Please forgive me."

Young Pablo stood up hesitantly, blushing as he took a furtive glance at Vanessa and Juliana. "I am sorry, my King, for turning on you. I just wanted to have . . . to have my own way instead of honoring you. All I have done has left me empty inside. Can you ever forgive me?"

Daniela smoothed her skirt and rose. Alonso struggled to his feet using the edge of the table. Olivia picked up Diego and held him in her arms. One by one, each person stood and expressed their sorrow over rebelling against the King, and they declared their earnest desire to be restored to his good graces.

At last the King himself stood, and, looking into the eyes of each person, he said, "Thank you, my dear friends. I love each of you, and I forgive you, and I restore you to myself."

"Thank you, my King," Rodrigo said, and everyone agreed.

"It is time for me to rebuild my Kingdom," the King said, "and I want each of you to be a part of it."

"That is our desire," Joaquin said. "Our lives have been unbearable apart from you."

"Our separation has grieved me as well," said the King. "And so, the first thing I ask of you is that you be with me. I am with you always, and I want to share in your lives and for you to share in my life with me. Soon, you will be tempted to think of me as a symbol, and you will want to teach object lessons inspired by me, and to institute rituals to represent me, and to celebrate festivals in honor of me. But know this: my Kingdom will not be built upon principles or practices or pageantry; it will be built upon me. Sharing in the life of my Kingdom will begin and end in sharing in my life. Walk with me, talk with me, work by my side; this is how you are to be a part of my Kingdom. This is important. Can you do this?"

"Yes, my King," Daniela said. "Communion with you is our very lifeblood." Everyone agreed.

"That is good," said the King. "And as you share in my life, I also ask you to honor me as the King of everything."

"You are the King, and we do honor you!" Felipe declared.

"Thank you," said the King, "and I am honored by you. But I am aware such commitments can easily falter. You have already rebelled against me once, claiming my Kingdom for yourselves. I do not say this to shame you or to open old wounds, but to recognize that your hearts are vulnerable to such temptations. There will be times you will want to reject my authority altogether, desiring to rule over your own lives. Other times, you will wish to give me reign over certain aspects of your lives while withholding other aspects for your own purposes. These temptations will come, but you must resist them. Embrace the truth of my being King, and honor my claim over everyone and everything. This also is important. Can you do this?"

"Yes, my King," Alonso said. "You are the one true King over everything." Everyone agreed.

"That is good," said the King. "And as you share in my life and honor me as the King of everything, I also ask you to live out my laws. Honor all others above yourselves, and honor me above all others."

"Your laws are good and true, my King," Olivia said as Diego squirmed in her arms. "We all have felt the heartache that comes when we forsake them."

"Yes," said the King. "I have grieved over the suffering each of you experienced as you honored yourselves above all others. And yet, such lessons are easily forgotten. There will be times when you are tempted to return to your selfish mindset and forsake my laws altogether. Other times, you will apply your cleverness to finding loopholes and exceptions, claiming to fulfill my laws while honoring yourselves above all others and me. Still other times, you will imagine that my laws only apply to those within my Kingdom, leaving you free to condemn, dishonor, and misuse those who have not yet been restored to me. But know this, I am the King of everyone and everything. You must honor all others above yourselves as you honor me above all others. Only by truly honoring my laws will peace be restored and your suffering be turned into joy. I have honored you above myself in all things, even to the point of receiving the full violence of your rebellion without retaliating against you. Learn from me: walk by my side and share in my love for you, and let me guide you and strengthen you as you live out my love for all others. This is most important of all. Can you do this?"

"Yes, my King," young Vanessa said with tears in her eyes. "We want nothing more than to walk with you and share in your love."

"That is good," the King said. "As you share in my life and live out my laws, you will grow in love and faithfulness together. Then your community will serve as a beacon, helping to guide others back to me and my Kingdom. This is my desire for you, and I am glad it is your desire as well. There is much to be done, and we will find joy in carrying out this work together."

"We rejoice that you have called us to share in your life and work, my King, and we are ready to join you in all you are doing," said Rodrigo. Everyone agreed.

"That is good," said the King. "And now, if I am not mistaken, I believe I smell Martina's famous churros. And is that cajeta sauce?"

"It is," Martina said with a smile.

"Then I think the next order of business should be for us to enjoy this delicious gift together!" the King declared. Everyone agreed.

Chapter 3

～

T hree men walked along the path in animated conversation. Each of their outward appearance and accented speech made it clear they were not locals, but it was the sheer joy of their comradery that caught the attention of the people around them. They laughed and exclaimed as they exchanged their news.

"That is extraordinary, Safi!" said a light-skinned man dressed in coat and trousers with an ascot tied around his neck. "And she was healed just like that?"

"Yes, it is true, Albert! I am a witness to it myself!" Safi replied. His deep olive complexion was accented by his cream-colored linen tunic and pants. "He took her hand and kissed it, and you could see the sores close, the scabs fade, and her skin become restored. Even the old scars disappeared, leaving behind supple, living flesh. It was a wonder!"

"A leper made whole," said the third man with a wide, bright grin. He was a head taller than the other two, and his rich, chocolatey skin was covered by a blue and purple robe hanging down from his broad shoulders. "I wonder what is next, the dead being raised?"

"I wouldn't put it past him, Irungu, my brother," Albert laughed. "He said he is rebuilding his Kingdom, and he isn't being subtle about it."

"Look, it is Zoya and Catalina!" said Safi, and the men turned to greet the two women who had been waving at them. One was a tiny woman whose black hair had streaks of white and whose back was bent with age. The other was young and tall, and her golden hair was pulled back in a braid.

"Ah, what a joy it is to see you all," the smaller woman said, her coppery face crinkled with a smile.

"It is good to see you, as well, my dear Catalina," said Irungu as he bent down to embrace her.

"Zoya! How are you?" Safi asked. "And how is your little Inessa? My Amir was asking about her just the other day!"

"She is very well, my friend," the blond woman said as she hugged each of the men. "And how is your beautiful Rana keeping herself?"

"Oh, you know, she always worries when I travel across the nations," Safi said. "But I tell her that is what faith is for."

"Ah, here are our compatriots!" said a man from across a swath of lawn.

"Jian! Amelie! You both made it!" exclaimed Catalina. "What a blessing it is for us all to be together again!"

"Yes!" said Amelie. "It is always a joy to gather with your brothers and sisters, no? But where is our host?"

The seven looked around. Above them towered tall buildings in every direction, and surrounding them were the trees, lawns, and paths of the vast park that sat in the middle of the great city. Hundreds of people were walking, jogging, and picnicking all about. The friends shook their heads with amusement as they attempted to spot the one who had called them together.

"He loves to do this to us," laughed Zoya.

"Yes," said Irungu. "He always keeps us guessing."

"There he is," Jian said, pointing. They followed his gaze and saw the King sitting on a bench surrounded by a flock of pigeons. He reached into a brown paper bag, and, to the pigeons' delight, he brought out a fist full of breadcrumbs and scattered them on the ground. With flapping wings and excited coos, the birds resumed their pecking.

"My King," said Safi, "you drag us all across the nations, then spend your time feeding pigeons?"

"Exactly," said the King. "I am the King of everything, after all, and they were hungry." He stood, shook out the bag, folded it up, and placed it in his pocket. "Now that that is done, let me look at you all."

He embraced each person. "Ah, Safi Hakim, Li Jian, Zoya Sokolov, Irungu Kamau, Catalina Suarez, Albert Davies, and, of course, Amelie Allard. My dear friends, thank you for traveling so far to join me. I know such a journey can be difficult, and that you are missed back in your own communities, but I believe there is value in such gatherings. Come, walk with me."

They followed the King as he strolled down the pathway. He looked with obvious appreciation at both the natural beauty and the human accomplishments standing all around them. His enthusiasm was infectious, and they found themselves seeing things in a new light.

"It is a joy to be with you," the King said as he walked. "I have spent time with each of you and the communities you represent. I am so pleased with the fellowship we share and the love you share together as my people. And I am pleased your communities are reaching out to each other, celebrating the bond you share together, and being a source of encouragement and inspiration for each other as you walk with me. All of this is very good."

"We are glad it pleases you, my King," Catalina said. "Before your return, I was so twisted up with selfishness that I did not even care about my own children. I never imagined I would become a part of a loving family that spans the nations! I find myself with more brothers and sisters than I can count. It is a joy beyond what my words can express."

"Yes," said Jian. "Thank you, my King, for sharing us with each other. Your love fills our hearts, and it is a great delight whenever we can be together."

"Of course, we spend much of our time talking about you," Safi said with a grin. "You truly are the glue that binds us together."

"All of this fills my heart with joy," said the King. "But know this: the bond we share together is not only for our own enjoyment, it serves an even greater purpose. I am rebuilding my Kingdom, and the time has come for you and the communities you represent to join me even further in my work. It is my intention to take the love, joy, and peace we share together, and to lift it up as a witness to the nations. You may not realize it, but what you are experiencing has become quite foreign to the rest of the world. It is an echo of the blessings everyone enjoyed with me before the rebellion, and everyone longs for those blessings deep in their heart once again. As you share together in the fullness of life with me, you bear witness to the truth that I am alive, and that I am offering love, forgiveness, and reconciliation to all, and that I long to welcome everyone back into the joy of my Kingdom. This is important. Can you do this?"

"But, yes, my King," said Amelie. "This is a beautiful vision of your Kingdom, and we are anxious to offer others the wonderful life we have with you."

"That is good," said the King. "Now, if you will excuse me . . ."

He stepped off the path, knelt down, crawled through a gap in a hedge, and disappeared.

The men and women looked at each other.

With a shrug, Albert said, "I'll go."

Scrambling after the King, he came into a wide clearing in the middle of a tall thicket. Around the circle were makeshift tents and pieces of trash strewn all about. In the midst of the clutter sat two bedraggled men, and an old woman who laid on her side clutching her stomach.

The King was holding one of the men's hand, and when he released it, the man found a loaf of bread on his palm. He gaped at it in wonder.

"Did you see that, Tom?"

"That I did, Bill!"

Next, the King picked up a discarded plastic shopping bag, and, one after another, he drew out a bottle of clear, golden liquid and round earthen cups, apples, oranges and grapes, a dish of steaming potatoes and a platter of roasted chicken. Then he extracted earthen plates and cloth napkins, and he laid it all out on a red-and-white checkered picnic blanket.

Bill and Tom laughed and began eating.

The King moved over to the woman. "Cynthia," he said, laying a hand on her mud and sweat smeared brow, "I have provided a feast for you. Would you like to eat of it?"

"Oh, my King," the old woman moaned, "I thank you, but I'm afraid I'm not fit to enjoy your gifts. My poor innards have been grieving me something fierce, and I haven't eaten for days."

"May I help you with that?" the King asked, stroking the old woman's hair.

"So kind," she groaned, "but I have been around long enough to know when something is beyond help."

The King smiled gently. "Cynthia Hutchins, do you not remember? I am the King of everything. I am your King, and I am the King of your innards, and I am the King over that which grieves you. I would very much like to help."

"Well, if it's not too much trouble, I would be most grateful," Cynthia said.

The King placed one hand on her back and gave her a comforting rub. Then he placed his other over the woman's hands as they gripped her belly.

"There," he said. "Is that any better?"

Cynthia blinked, then sat up and probed her stomach with her fingers. "My King," she exclaimed, "it's gone! The pain and gnawing are gone! Sakes alive, I never could've dreamt it!"

The King received her hugs and kisses with pleasure. "I told you I am the King of everything," he said, laughing.

"Ma!" said Tom. "How about a drumstick and a tater?"

"Gladly," she said, and took the proffered plate from her son.

"William, Thomas, and Cynthia," the King said, "it is good to be with you as ever. I will see you again soon."

"Thank you, my King, for everything," Tom said, and the small party raised their cups in salute.

The King crawled back out of the hedge, and Albert followed after him. Brushing off dirt and twigs, they rejoined the group.

"What was that about?" asked Zoya.

"An appointment," said the King, and he continued down the path.

"I'll tell you later," said Albert as they ran to keep up.

"Now," resumed the King, "as you nurture the strength of your own communities, and as you continue to build relationships with all my followers across the nations, it is imperative you reach out to the people around you as well. Since the rebellion, selfishness has been the driving force within everyone's heart and mind. This has stirred up pride, greed, and envy, and hatred, conflict, and war have been the inevitable result. The powerful compete for ever more power, while the powerless are exploited, beaten down, and crushed. Everyone is in a state of perpetual discontentment, and misery, fear, and despair grip the hearts of many."

"Yes, my King," Irungu said with a sigh. "We see great suffering all around us."

"I am the King of everything, and everyone you see belongs to me," said the King. "I know each one by name, and their suffering grieves my heart. As I rebuild my Kingdom, I am at work offering healing, support, and care to the lost and broken, and I want you to join me in this endeavor. I have shared my love with you, strengthened you, and supplied all your needs. Now, take what I have given you and share it with all those around you. Feed the hungry, heal the sick, welcome the wanderer, liberate the oppressed. Work by my side and demonstrate my goodness so the lost may be found, the broken may be restored, and those who despair may rediscover hope. This is so important, my friends. Will you join me in this?"

"You are our King," said Catalina. "Your heart is our heart, and your desires shape the mission of our lives. We will join you in this work."

"Thank you," the King said. He stopped walking and turned to look each of his friends in the eye. "I warn you," he said, "there will be resistance. Through our work together, we will expose the folly of the rebellion, and many will reject their arrogance, greed, and hatred and return to me. But the powerful will want to hold onto their power, and the nations will not want to set aside their sovereignty. As you take your stand for me and my Kingdom, you will be recognized as a threat to the new order of things. They will attempt to persuade you and control you, and if they are unsuccessful, they will seek to slander you and crush you. And yet, even in this, you will bear witness to my goodness and expose their folly. This, too, is important. Can you do this for me?"

"Yes, my King," Safi said, taking Jian's hand in his right and Zoya's in his left. They all formed a circle. "You are the King of everything, and you are a good King. With you there is life, and apart from you there is only emptiness, misery, and death. We love you, and though we abandoned you once, we are devoted to you now and forever. We will face whatever hardship comes our way as we join you in your invaluable work." Everyone agreed.

"That is good," said the King. "There is much for us to do. And now, I believe I see a vendor who will put a hot dog on a stick, dip it in corn batter, and deep fry it until it is golden brown and crunchy. With mustard, these things are surprisingly good. Who will join me for a quick bite?" They all followed him along the path toward the cart.

Part II

~

As more and more were restored to the King, they began to share in His work. They reached out to the people around them, bearing witness to the King's return and extending his invitation of restoration.

Chapter 1

～

T he man slowly dislodged the items he held tightly in his arms and placed each one carefully on the counter. The shopkeeper watched the process with amusement, wondering over the wild assortment of foods his customer had selected. There was a jar of tart green olives and a container of curdled cottage cheese, a stick of spicy beef jerky and a bag of chocolate covered mints, a bottle of marinara sauce and a box of almond cookies. Lastly, he lowered a jar of dill pickle spears and a half-gallon of mocha swirl ice cream.

"I am painfully aware of the cliché," the man said, smiling, "but what can you do?"

"How far along is she?" asked the shopkeeper.

"We've got a month to go," the man said. "Too far and way too close at the same time. It's terrifying."

The shopkeeper laughed. "I'm sure you'll do fine, a young guy like you!"

"Thanks, Amar, I appreciate your vote of confidence!"

The shopkeeper blinked. "You know my name?"

"Well, sure. I've been coming to your store for two months now."

"I'm sorry to say I don't know your name," said Amar.

"That's alright," the man said, grinning. "You've got to have, what, hundreds of customers, and I've only got one of you! Oh, and my name is Steve."

"It is good to officially meet you, Steve," Amar said. "But, really, no one knows anyone's name. Everyone is too busy."

"I guess so," Steve said. "I've been making a point of trying to remember peoples' names. You know, 'Honor all others above yourself.'"

"Oh," said Amar, frowning. "The old King's law. How provincial. I heard some are claiming he's alive. It's utter nonsense, of course!"

"No, it's the real deal. I've seen him," said Steve.

"Wait, what?" asked Amar. "You've seen him?"

"Sure," Steve said. "Actually, I see him a lot. We meet up and go for walks and talk and stuff. My wife and I gather with neighbors and friends and spend time with him together, too. It's been great."

"You seem like a sane man," Amar said. "I wouldn't tell too many people about your delusions."

Steve laughed. "Yeah, it's okay, I'm not too worried about that. All I can say is, things have been really different since the King came back. Just being with him, listening to him, and seeing how he treats everybody, it has really turned me around. I'll be honest, I used to be a complete jerk. I was terrible to my wife, horrible to my neighbors, and a real cutthroat at the office. But seeing how much the King loves me and values me has made all my insecurities and ambitions feel a lot less important. And, I have to tell you, actually loving and honoring the people around me has been a million times better than just thinking about myself. Life has become bigger, richer, and far more interesting. And now I've got a little one on the way. I'm ashamed to say it, but, at first, I felt resentful of everything the kid was going to demand of me; but now, since I reconnected with the King, I'm actually excited about doing whatever I can to help make his or her life as amazing as possible. And the greatest thing is, I know all of this is honoring the King. This is exactly what he's always wanted for us: to feel loved by him and to love each other like he loves us. So, yeah, I'd say life is good!"

"Well, I envy you," Amar said, shaking his head. "My wife is a nag, constantly talking about all the things she wants, never listening to me about what I want. And my kids are nothing but leeches, always taking and taking from me, but never giving anything in return. I am glad everything has turned out so great for you."

"It isn't me," Steve said, "it's the King. I am anything but perfect now, and I constantly get caught up in my own selfishness, but he's teaching me, and I'm starting to make some progress. My life is truly better."

"That's good, that's good," said Amar. "I see a sparkle in your eye that I used to have a long, long time ago. Before everything changed. Before . . . you know."

"Sure. Well, it's nice to hear you can see something different in me. That's encouraging. But I want you to know there's not a single thing that's special about me. It's a reflection of him, and he loves you just as much as he loves me. He's pulling his Kingdom back together, and I know for a fact he wants you to be a part of it."

"You've given me a lot to think about," Amar said as he placed the last item into the bag.

Steve paid him. "It's good to talk with you! Now I better get the ice cream and pickles back to the wife before she eats something really disgusting!"

"Good luck with everything, Steve!"

"Thanks, Amar! I'll see you soon!"

The shopkeeper put the bills and coins into his cash register and wiped the ring of condensation left by the ice cream off the counter. "What a funny guy," he said under his breath. "A little crazy in the head, but nice."

Chapter 2

~

T he man eyed the building suspiciously, squinting at its simple design and clean exterior. *Harrumph*, he thought to himself and jotted a note on his pad.

He had been standing across the street for an hour, watching a steady stream of people coming and going through the front doors of the establishment. He was bothered by the wide diversity of its clientele, people of obvious wealth and social prominence walking through the same doors as people of poverty and insignificance. He saw a businessman dressed in a tailored suit hold the door for an old man dressed in little more than rags. *Harrumph*, he thought again, and made another note.

At last, he stepped off the curb and marched across the street. He pushed open one of the doors and began to enter, but, in his rush, he bumped into a young woman carrying a bag of rice in one arm and a swaddled infant in another. Behind her were two small children, one hefting a bag of melons and the other cradling a live chicken in her arms.

"Watch where you are going," he said, scowling at the woman.

"Thank you," said the woman with a smile, and she and her children passed through the door he still held open.

"Harrumph," he said out loud, and taking one last contemptuous look at the family, he turned and entered the building.

What he saw was a buzzing hive of activity. Within a large reception area, a wide array of people moved about in every direction. Men and women gathered around various kiosks and desks distributed across the lobby, and many others stood in lines filing through numerous doorways. Posters, placards, and banners labeled everything, and arrowed signboards offered further directions down numerous hallways. He saw that some of the people milling about wore badges, and he stepped in front of a man whose tag read "Emem Omezi: Foster Services."

"Do you work here?" he asked.

Emem struggled to avoid colliding with him. "Why, yes, I do!" he said, smiling. "How may I help you, sir?"

"I demand to speak with the person in charge. I understand it is a Mrs. Amara Nnamdi?"

"Yes," Emem said, his smile broadening. "We are very blessed to have Amara as our director. She is a gifted woman! I am uncertain where she may be at this moment, but I would be happy to track her down for you. May I say who is asking for her?"

"Yes," said the man. "Tell her it is Inspector Edozie from the Ministry. And tell her I am here to perform a review of this operation, and that it would be to everyone's advantage if I was not kept waiting."

"Thank you, Inspector Edozie," Emem said. "Why don't you stand here, and I will locate Amara for you. It shouldn't take long."

Inspector Edozie scowled, but nodded his consent. As Emem hurried away, he continued his observations of the business being conducted around him. He looked at some of the plaques over the office doors and read "Housing Assistance," "Employment Services," and "Legal Advocacy." One hallway was marked by an arrowed sign labeled "Community Pantry," and another with "Community Closet." He scribbled it all onto his pad.

"You must be Inspector Edozie," a voice said, and he turned to see a small woman dressed in a simple beige suit and white shirt. Her hair was tightly woven into dozens of braids that were gathered and bound into a wild-looking ponytail. She held out her hand to him.

"Director Nnamdi?" he asked, looking at her hand as if it was covered in grime.

"Yes, but, please," she said, "call me Amara. And what is your name?"

"As you said," he sneered, "I am Inspector Edozie."

She smiled. "Inspector what Edozie?"

He frowned. "My name is Inspector Dayo Edozie."

"See," she laughed, patting him on the shoulder, "that wasn't so hard. Now, Dayo, what may I do for you?"

He backed up a step, looking perturbed. "I am from the Ministry's Department of Civil Concerns, and we are concerned about reports we have received regarding your organization. I am here to initiate a full investigation."

"I am sorry to hear the Ministry is troubled over us," Amara said, "but I feel confident that once you see what we are accomplishing here, you will be able to bring back a positive report. I have much to do, but I would be happy to show you around as I go. Would that be alright?"

"I suppose it would be unreasonable to expect your full attention," Dayo said, "so, yes, that will have to do."

"I am glad," Amara said, giving him another pat. "Now, why don't you follow me."

She was instantly in motion, working her way around the spacious lobby. She greeted an elderly woman and hugged a small child. She gave a form to a man whose badge said "Lekan Ebujo: Volunteer" and asked a question of another worker sitting behind a desk. She pinned several announcements onto a giant bulletin board and picked up a piece of trash from the floor. In a matter of moments, Amara worked her way around the entire reception area, interacting with dozens of people and accomplishing numerous tasks. Dayo struggled to keep up with her.

"Hmm," she said, coming to a stop. "Monifa wanted me to stop by her office, and the food pantry was running low on bags, but first I must go over to the medical clinic," she told him. "It's a short walk down the street. Do you mind? It will give us a chance to talk away from all the noise. The acoustics are terrible in this room, don't you think?"

Dayo frowned as he sorted through everything she had said. "Yes, I suppose there is a lot of noise here, and, no, I do not mind accompanying you to the clinic. That is an operation I especially want to examine."

"Good," she said. "Thank you for your patience." She pushed her way through the front doors, holding one open for Dayo, and began descending the building's steps. "How familiar are you with our history?" she asked as they strode down the sidewalk.

"I am not familiar with it at all," he grudgingly admitted.

"Well, it started with a few of us wanting to do something kind for our neighbors. We had been meeting with the King . . ."

"Excuse me?" Dayo asked, his voice rising an octave. "The King?" He pulled out his pad and pen.

"Yes," Amara said with a gentle smile. "He had contacted each of us, and then he brought us together. We formed a little family. It was lovely."

"But the King is dead," Dayo stated decisively.

"Oh, that's silly," Amara laughed, "I just spoke with him an hour ago. Anyway, we were all together enjoying a meal and telling each other what we had been up to that day. When it was the King's turn, he shared about how he had fed an impoverished family, tended to an injured stone worker, and visited with a widow who lives on my own street. They all seemed like very good things to do, and we said we would like to join the King in helping the people who live around us. He was delighted. Our efforts started small: delivering a meal to someone here, offering a ride to someone there. Then we expanded a little: collecting spare clothing, organizing activities for the neighborhood children, visiting with people unable to leave their homes. We discovered there is a great deal of poverty all around us in the city and surrounding villages, and there is so much loneliness. We joined the King in finding more and more ways to help address the needs of our neighbors, and he brought more and more people to work with us. Some of them were wealthy, and, with their support, we were able to purchase our main building back there, as well as the health clinic, the orphanage, and the school. We are working towards establishing a shelter to help our city's homeless population, and another clinic to help people overcome their addictions. It is a very exciting time! Ah, here we are."

They came to a single-storied concrete building with a sign reading "Community Medical Clinic." Men, women, and children stood in line outside its doors. Amara greeted several of them, asking a mother about her infant, affectionately squeezing an old man's shoulder, and laughing with a teenaged boy.

"Unfortunately, we do not have enough space in the reception area for everyone," she told Dayo as they stepped up to the entrance.

A young woman dressed in a blue medical smock opened the door for them. "Hello, Amara!" she said. "It is so good to see you!"

Amara gave her a hug. "It is very good to see you, too, Chinwe! This is my friend, Inspector Edozie from the Ministry."

"I am happy to meet you," Chinwe said.

"Yes," Dayo said with a stiff nod.

"Chinwe is one of our triage nurses," Amara told him. "She interviews each person who comes to us and determines their level of need. Those who are in danger, we bring back immediately; those who are hurting and weak, we have sit in reception; and those who are able, we have wait outside. It is not ideal, but we are doing what we can."

They entered the building and Dayo's eyes widened for a moment as he saw how many people filled the chairs of the spacious waiting room.

"Follow me," Amara said, and they skirted around the edge to the doors leading to the medical services beyond. "Ah, Okoro," she said as she saw a tall man in a green smock. "Good to see you, my friend!"

"Amara!" Okoro said, leaning down and giving her a hug. "I am glad you are here."

"Yes," she said. "Yakuba said you needed to speak with me?"

"I do," he said, straightening up and looking around them, "but this is not the place. Could you wait in my office for me? I have a patient to see, but then we can talk together. It should only be a few minutes."

"Of course," Amara said, patting Okoro's arm, "we will see you soon." She turned to Inspector Edozie, "Come, Dayo, I will give you a little tour of the clinic while we wait for Dr. Nwosu."

"I would appreciate it," he said, taking in everything around him.

"This is the nurses' station. It serves as the hub for all medical activities in the clinic." There was a long counter running along a battery of cabinets and desks where several nurses sat juggling files and conferring with the doctors, nurses, and technicians that streamed past them.

Amara led the Inspector around the corner and down a hallway. There were doors on both sides, most of which had a file resting in a holder attached to the wall beside it. "These are the clinic's examination rooms." She found one that did not have a file, knocked, and opened the door. Inside, there were cabinets, a sink, a waste container, chairs, and a short, padded table. The room was painted in warm colors. "Most of our patients are brought to one of these rooms for diagnosis and treatment. We have tried to make them as comfortable as possible."

She closed the door and they continued down the hall, passing doctors, nurses, and patients as they went. She led him through a set of double doors.

"This is the diagnostic center of the clinic," she said. "We house our own laboratory and two X-ray machines, which save a great deal of time and expense for our patients. And through those doors is our surgery center. We have three fully-equipped theaters."

They went down another hallway and came into a wide room divided into individual stalls by curtains running along tracks set in the ceiling. "This is the immediate care section of the clinic where people who are experiencing medical emergencies are treated."

A man in a green smock walked by and said, "Hello, Director Nnamdi." His facial features and accented tones showed he was from the east.

"Hello, Dr. Nakamura," she said. "This is Inspector Edozie from our government's Ministry. I am giving him a tour of our clinic."

"It is very good to meet you, Inspector," the doctor said with a slight bow.

"Hiroki is here on loan from his own nation," Amara said.

"Yes," he said, "the King asked me to come, and so I came."

"The King?" Dayo asked, an eyebrow raised.

"Why, yes," Hiroki said and laughed. "Believe me, I would not have left my home for any other reason. But I am glad my skills can be of help here. He dearly loves these people, and because of that, I love them, too."

Dayo wrote on his pad.

"Good to see you, Dr. Nakamura," Amara said, and they moved on.

She led them across the room to a door that opened into yet another hallway. "These are the offices for our physicians and surgeons."

Dr. Nwosu stuck his head out of one of the doors. "Ah! There you are! Come in, come in!"

When they stepped into the office, the doctor looked between them awkwardly. "Amara, I . . . I have something very important to discuss with you, but it requires the utmost confidentiality. I am not questioning the Inspector's integrity, but . . ."

"It's alright, Okoro," Amara said. "He is from the Ministry, and whatever we do, we must be an open book in front of him."

"Very well," Okoro said as he shut the door behind them. "Please, take a seat. Actually, it could be advantageous that the Inspector is here: he might be able to help us make the necessary connections with the Ministry."

"What is this about?" asked Amara.

"Though I have been serving here as a general physician, my background is in infectious diseases," Okoro said. "I gave epidemiology special attention in my studies at medical school, and, a few years ago, I served on a taskforce that dealt with an outbreak of the pox. I tell you this so you will recognize the weight of what I have to say. Over the past few weeks, we have had a number of children brought in for treatment. They were very ill, with their primary symptoms being a severe headache, high fever, and stiffness of the neck. I tested them and was able to diagnose that they suffered from bacterial meningitis. I prescribed the necessary antibiotics, and they all showed signs of improvement within days. Unfortunately, several more cases have come in from the city, with both children and adults infected, and, today, two children were brought in from an outlying village. I fear we are facing an epidemic."

Amara looked intently into his eyes. "What can we do?"

"As I said, treatment is relatively easy, but our own supply of the necessary antibiotics is very limited. Also, we do not have anywhere near the number of people it would take to adequately screen both the city's population and the neighboring villages. And there needs to be communication with the populace so people can take the necessary precautions. All that to say, this really does require the Department of Health's involvement."

"Have you spoken with the King about this?" asked Amara.

"It was his idea to involve the Ministry," Okoro said. "He said it is important to use all the tools available to us, and they have the necessary resources to both treat the number of people likely to be infected and help contain the spread of the illness. And, well, you know him," he laughed. "He said he is the King of everything, and that includes the Ministry."

Dayo snorted, then looked at the others. "That is an empty claim," he said, frowning.

"Not from what I've seen," Amara said. "Very well, I will contact the Department of Health. Do you have your documentation compiled?"

"Yes," Okoro said, handing her a packet. "And I wrote up my projections."

"Dayo," she said, "would you be willing to deliver this to Minister Amadi? I will call his office, but it would add weight if you personally represented this conversation to him."

He looked at the director and the doctor through narrowed eyes, taking each of their measure. "Yes," he said at last, "I will bring your information to Amadi, but I can make no promises. He is a proud man, and a lazy man, though you did not hear that from me. But, if what you say is true, then clearly action needs to be taken. I will speak with Simisola Metu, his Under-Secretary. She will know how to manage him."

"Very well," Okoro said, standing, "I am satisfied. I will continue to address the situation from here, and I will communicate any new developments. In the meantime, we will see what the King will do through our efforts."

"I'll speak with him," Amara said, "and I'll let you know what Minister Amadi says. Thank you for your faithfulness, Okoro."

"And thank you for yours, Amara," he said. "And for your assistance, Inspector Edozie."

"Yes, Dr. Nwosu," Dayo said, "it . . . it is the right thing to do."

Amara led him through the hallways and out of the clinic. "I am sorry to cut our time short, Dayo," she said as they hurried up the sidewalk, "but I must give this new situation my immediate attention."

"I understand," said the Inspector.

"May I ask, what is your impression of our organization so far?"

"Yes," he said, "that is a very good question. To be honest, I am disturbed not only by your insistence that a dead man is alive, but by your giving him the allegiance that belongs solely to the Ministry and our nation as a whole. These concerns are heightened by the fact that you consort with foreigners and have them serve roles your own countrymen are capable of fulfilling. I am left questioning your loyalty and, frankly, wondering if you are traitors to your nation and a threat to its people."

Amara laughed, "Well, that does not sound like a very favorable impression."

"No," he said, "it does not. And yet . . . and yet it is clear you are sincerely working to serve the needs of the people of this city. Even from my brief observations, I can see you are all motivated by something greater than the selfishness that drives the rest of us. You say it comes from your relationship with the old King, which is absurd; and yet, it is coming from something you all share, and the results are obvious. You may be traitors, but, ironically, your treachery might be the very thing we need the most. For now, I will withhold my judgment."

"You make us sound like quite an enigma!" Amara said. "I only wish it was that exciting. But, thank you, Dayo, for your open mind. And thank you so much for your help! I pray I can catch Minister Amadi in a better mood than usual, and that we can stop the momentum of this disease."

"Yes, Amara," he said, and he held out his hand to her, "as do I."

She took it, then pulled him in and gave him a hug. "May the King bless you," she said.

"I don't . . ." he said, then laughed. "Very well, may the King bless me! I will speak with you soon!"

They parted in pursuit of a common purpose.

Chapter 3

∾

T he assembly hall was vast. Wood paneled walls stood sixty feet tall and elaborate chandeliers hung from the ceiling.

"Thank you, President Saunders," Moderator Legrand said from behind the podium on the stage. "We will give your proposal our most serious attention tonight and cast our votes tomorrow. And now, we have a report from Prime Minister Chu of the New Republic."

A man dressed in a gray double-breasted suit and coral silk necktie climbed the steps to the stage. "Thank you, Moderator. I believe I speak for everyone when I express my appreciation for your facilitating this great Summit of Nations with such wisdom and tact."

"Very kind, Honorable Chu," the tall man said, and after bowing, he took his seat.

"My friends," Prime Minister Chu said, speaking into the microphone, "a new day has dawned. This is a time of great prosperity for each of our nations. It is a pleasure to report that the illustrious New Republic has surpassed its projections for mass market productivity. Our engineers continue to create innovative ways to manufacture goods, and our builders continue to follow their designs in the construction of factories, and our workers continue to dedicate themselves to producing the greatest quantity of affordable merchandise available. The Merchant has assisted us in establishing trade agreements with a number of other nations for supplying the raw materials we need for production. They are clearcutting their forests for timber and dredging their rivers for ore, as well as strip-mining their hills for coal, drilling their oceans for oil, and fracking gasses out of the depths of the earth below them. The New Republic is taking all these resources and using them to fill the shelves of your markets, strip malls, and homes with goods at low, low prices! You will find our report in your files, along with forms for placing your orders."

The delegates applauded as the Prime Minister made a deep bow and left the stage.

"Thank you, Honorable Chu," Legrand said. "I have no doubt we will all benefit from the New Republic's efforts. I now recognize Lord Chancellor Schmidt of the United Federation."

A man in a black military uniform with multi-colored regalia stepped up to the stage. "Moderator," he said, giving Legrand a stiff bow. Turning, he bowed to the audience, "Distinguished leaders. My solitary goal in attending this Summit of Nations is the formation of alliances in my campaign against the Confederacy of Sovereign States. As you know, the rebel Otto Muench has broken away from the United Federation and positioned himself as a despotic overlord in defiance of my rule. And, what is more, he has rallied a number of the nations along my borders against me, and his Confederacy continues to grow in size and strength. A great war is imminent, which poses a threat to us all. The Merchant has assisted the United Federation in amassing armaments and munitions, and we have conscripted the troops needed to put them to their proper use, but I fear it will not be enough. I appeal to you to ally your nations with me and to join in my fight, and together we will defend the freedoms we all hold dear against the tyranny of Muench. I will be holding a meeting in the boardroom immediately following this session. I urge you to attend."

The men and women in the audience shifted in their seats and glanced surreptitiously at each other with subtle signs and gestures.

"Difficult business, Lord Chancellor, to be sure," Legrand said. "I now call Grand Chairman Jamal of the People's Commonwealth to the podium." At the mention of Jamal's name, the tension in the room broke and the dignitaries erupted with applause.

A heavyset man dressed in a long, ornamented blue robe and wearing dark tinted spectacles bounded up the steps to the stage. With jeweled rings sparkling on each of his fingers, he waved both his hands at the crowd. "Please, please, you all know me!" he said into the microphone. "Grand Chairman? Ha! I am your friend, Farooq!"

More cheers and laughter came from the tables.

"Yes, and what a beautiful crowd you are!" Farooq said with a grin. "It is with great pleasure that I stand here, and it is great pleasure I offer. Our friends in the New Republic carry on their business, and the United Federation fights its wars, but what are business and wars for if not to have a good time at the end of the day?"

One dignitary whistled, and all the rest laughed.

"The People's Commonwealth has been working with the Merchant to offer you rest and relaxation, and diversions of every sort," Farooq continued. "Our exotic resorts provide lounging along the beach and pampering in our spas, as well as exciting activities for the whole family. And our pleasure palaces proffer sumptuous feasts, dazzling entertainments, and games of chance throughout the day, along with voluptuous revelries throughout the night. We can supply you with amusement parks and circuses, food festivals and wine tasting tours, luxury cruises and catered safaris. Whatever your fancy, we will indulge you."

The heads of state enthusiastically applauded the Grand Chairman.

"Thank you, yes!" he said. "But I have saved the best for last: a new invention the Merchant himself has engineered for us. In just one month, we will begin providing entertainments that may be enjoyed in the homes of each and every one of your nations' people! He has designed boxes that project sounds and images, and your people will be able to watch moving, talking pictures depicting everything from the antics of mischievous clowns to the passions of uninhibited lovers to the violence of rampaging psychopaths. Their programming will lull your people into complacency, providing excellent opportunities to stir up their discontentment while advertising your products for the stimulation of your economies. My write-up is included in your papers. Let the People's Commonwealth cater to your every desire!"

Again, the Grand Chairman raised his hands and waved at the crowd, and they responded with hoots, hollers, and raucous cheers as he descended from the stage.

Legrand stared down at the itinerary in his hand. "I am uncertain how this has happened," he said, frowning, "but scheduled next is an address from someone named Mrs. Myrtle Merriweather." He looked out at the audience. "It says she is here as a representative of the Old Dominion."

A sudden hush fell upon the great room. Many of the delegates narrowed their eyes, curled back their lips, and hissed as a little white-haired woman draped in a mint green dress hobbled up the steps to the stage. When she stood behind the podium, her eyes barely peeked over its edge.

"If you don't mind, dear," she said to Legrand with a tentative smile.

"Oh, yes, of course," he said, flustered, and pulled down an additional riser from behind the lectern.

Mrs. Merriweather stepped up and became visible to the audience. "Thank you, dear," she said. "That's much better."

"Not at all," Legrand said, and stepped back.

The woman looked out at the audience. Leaning into the microphone, she said, "Hello!" and her voice boomed across the auditorium with a screech of feedback. "Oh my!" she said, quickly pulling back. "As the nice man said, I am Mrs. Merriweather, and I am here in the name of the King. I know many of you like to use the phrase Old Dominion, but it isn't very accurate, is it? For the King's dominion isn't old at all; it is a reality here and now. He is alive, and he was, is, and always will be the King of everything."

Grumblings and rumblings issued from the audience.

"Yes, yes, I understand," Mrs. Merriweather said in a matronly tone. "You have clearly enjoyed your time as presidents, prime ministers, and viziers. You have played at being kings and queens yourselves, truth be told, but I have come with an invitation from the one true King. He says the time has come for you to lay down

your paper crowns and return to him. He is rebuilding his Kingdom, and he dearly wants you to fully participate in its life."

The delegates pounded the tables with their fists and hurled
insults at the little old woman on the stage.

"This would require some significant changes," she said into
the microphone, "and change is difficult. But, really, are things at
present as good as all that? I listened to your speeches, and you
paint a pretty picture, but there is much you have left unspoken.
You celebrate your economic prosperity, but you fail to speak of
the lying, cheating, and stealing that feeds your greed, and the perpetual poverty that keeps your people under your thumb, let alone
the rampant consumerism that dominates our lives with mounting
debt and discontentment. You boast of your military prowess, but
you gloss over the arrogance and hatred that drives you forward,
as well as the pain and fear that your ambitions bring down upon
us. And all the while, you dangle amusements to enslave us to
our petty desires and distract us from the misery that plagues our
world. Each one of us has honored ourselves above all others, and
it has left us broken, divided, and in despair.

"Do you remember what it was like?" she asked. "Do you
remember the peace and the joy we experienced under the King's
rule? It is a powerful thing to be loved, and the King knew each
one of us by name and cherished us all. We were able to put our full
confidence in him, trusting in the fact that he would always honor
us above himself. From his own larders he fed us in the midst of
famine, and within his own palace he sheltered us when floods
took our homes, and with his own power he healed us as plagues
ravaged our world. And when we all banded together and revolted
against his reign, he took the full brunt of our selfishness upon
himself, giving his life for us instead of exacting the justice we all
deserved. The King loved us so much, he gave us the chance to see
what life would be like without him. We have seen it, and it does
not measure up to the life we had with him.

"But now he is back. He is restoring his Kingdom, and he
is inviting us to once again share in his love and live out his love

together. He wants each one of us to honor all others above ourselves, to honor him above all others, and to be a part of the good
work he is doing.

"But know this," Mrs. Merriweather said, her voice dropping
an octave and cracking with the strain. "The King needs you to
understand that while his invitation is open to all, the hour is
coming when it will close. He granted us our time of rebellion,
and he is now gracing us with an opportunity for restoration, but
soon he will act to establish his Kingdom finally and absolutely.
He is the King of everything, and he loves his Kingdom too much
to allow it to suffer indefinitely the injuries, injustices, and despair
that our pride, greed, and hatred have wrought upon it. The day of
reckoning is coming, and those who pledge their allegiance to the
King will be fully restored to his Kingdom and enjoy its blessings,
but those who persist in their defiance of his rule will be disarmed
and exiled to a place where their selfishness will not disrupt the
life he will provide for his subjects.

"I understand your resistance. I do! I, myself, carried my best
butcher knife up that hill as we converged on the King. But I have
seen the error of my ways. The world we constructed for ourselves
parades our folly around and around every moment of every day,
and I, for one, am weary of it. My soul longs for something better,
something pure, something true. I remember the goodness our
good King shared with us, and now I am experiencing it again.
I beg you: let go of your pride, your greed, and your hatred, and
open your hearts to his love. This is his greatest desire for you. Be
reconciled to him, please, before it is too late."

Fishing out a handkerchief from her pocketbook, Mrs. Merriweather wiped her eyes and blew her nose. Amidst utter silence,
she shuffled across the stage, hobbled down the steps, and made
her way out of the auditorium.

The sound of the door clicking shut behind her seemed to
break a spell, and the premiers, chancellors, and chief executives
erupted with shouts of protest.

Moderator Legrand stepped to the microphone and raised his hands, "Ladies and gentlemen, please; some decorum, if you will. I believe a thirty-minute recess is in order. Go collect yourselves, and when you return, be prepared to get on with business as usual."

Part III

~

A s the King continued working with his people to rebuild his Kingdom, the nations became increasingly defiant.

Chapter 1

∽

M ore and more, the King's people reached out to those around them. They cared for the needs of their neighbors, they challenged injustices within their communities, and they extended the King's invitation of restoration. As more and more people embraced his invitation and turned their hearts back to him, their leaders grew more and more resentful.

∽

Within the village of Wawotu, Angga and Kemala Rahman were restored to the King. They were so pleased with the joy and peace they experienced, they began telling all their neighbors about his love. Many saw for themselves that the King was indeed alive and they could return to the life they had known with him, and they devoted themselves to his Kingdom.

Rimbo Anwar, the village chief, came to Angga and Kemala and rebuked them. "What are you doing, you two?" he demanded. "You are spreading lies and stirring up the people against me with your fairy tales! I am surprised at you, Angga, for you are an elder of this village!"

"No, Rimbo," said Angga, "these are not lies. The King is alive, and he is restoring his Kingdom."

"Yes, Chief Anwar," Kemala said, "it is true. And we so dearly want our whole village to share in the joy of his love and to know the peace they can have with him."

"This is foolishness," Rimbo spat. "You are in defiance of my rightful place as chief and the proper authority of our elders."

"You are chief," said Angga, "and the elders rule over our village, but he is the King of everything."

Rimbo Anwar called Wawotu's elders together, and they voted against Angga and Kemala and those who had responded to their message. They stripped Angga of his title and cast him and his family out of the village, and they threatened all those who pledged allegiance to the King with the same treatment. But more people devoted their lives to the King.

∾

Within the city of New Hartford, several communities of the King's people were founded, and they sought to honor all others above themselves as they honored the King above all others.

When Mayor Thompson and the rest of the city council heard of this, they began to take measures to halt the spread of the movement. They called the King's people "Misplaced Loyalists," "Old Dominians," "Superstitious Buffoons," and any other derogatory label they could come up with. They published articles in the papers slandering known Loyalists, and they spread rumors around the city that Old Dominians practiced secret rites and plotted insurrectionist attacks. They encouraged the New Hartford citizenry to boycott trade with any of the King's people in their community and to exclude them from their social circles.

"I don't understand, Mayor Thompson," Gary Richards said. "Why have you stirred up the people against us?"

"Because you and your fellow Loyalists are a threat to the public order of our fine city," Thompson said.

"But how could loving our neighbors and seeking their good above our own be a threat?"

"Because of whose name you do it in," Thompson said, "and because of the confusion it brings to the general populace. New Hartford is one of the major metropolitan centers in our great nation, which is one of the leading nations in our world, and our world runs on the superior principles of self-interest and healthy competition. Your constant appeal to the King and his Kingdom threatens the freedoms we hold dear, and all your talk of honoring others above yourself throws a giant monkey wrench into the innerworkings of our society. It is in the name of the greater good that we oppose you."

Gary sighed, "I honestly haven't seen much good since we revolted against the King, greater or otherwise. We lost so much on that day, and he is offering it all back and more. I've seen him, Your Honor, and I've heard his voice. I've walked with him and talked with him, and I've laughed with him and eaten meals with him. He is alive and he loves us, and he so dearly wants to share his life with us. Please, Mayor Thompson, know this: he is going to restore his Kingdom once and for all. This will happen, and it will happen soon, and he wants you and everyone else to be a part of it with him. But we all must turn from our rebellion and embrace him as our King. This is the only way, Your Honor."

Mayor Thompson's face had grown pale and his eyes were red-rimmed, but he shook himself and scowled. "See? This is what I'm talking about! You people prattle on and on about your pie-in-the-sky daydreams, and you try to push the rest of us off balance and pull us into your cause. But, I can assure you, it isn't going to work with me! I have had enough of your interference and fearmongering! I will be calling the city council together to consider what further actions we can take against you and your kind. And, believe you me, I will exercise the full measure of what is within my power! Now, go away! I am sick of the very sight of you!"

Pressures increased against those who were called Loyalists and Dominians and Buffoons, but still more people dedicated their lives to the King.

∽

Across the world, the followers of the King continued to grow in numbers. They encouraged and supported each other as they honored the King and refused to participate in the unjust practices of the nations.

"I am sorry, Secretary Gutierrez," Daniella Espinoza said, "but I cannot buy or sell this clothing. Those who produced it were exploited for their labors, and the materials they used were harvested by slaves. The King does not want me to profit from such things, and so I must decline."

"I apologize, General Lwanga," Mukisa Akello said, "but I cannot fight in your war. You have conscripted soldiers from across our nation and are forcing them to invade our weaker neighbors for your own gain. The King opposes my taking up arms in such an unjust campaign, and so I must refuse."

"Please forgive me, President Onasis," Endora Samaras said, "but I cannot be a party to these entertainments. The characters, plots, and images they present stir up pride, hatred, and lust, and they bring no glory to our King. He does not want me to seek enjoyment from such corruption, nor to promote it, and so I must excuse myself."

Over and over, the leaders of the nations found their agendas opposed by the followers of the King, and their strength and influence began to wane. Finally, they issued decrees banning all reference to the King and declared that anyone who claimed loyalty to his Kingdom would be considered a traitor to the state. They began to arrest his people, to beat and torture them, and to imprison them as they awaited trial for treason. The air was filled with their cries and smoke from their burning houses. Their suffering increased in breadth and intensity, but still more and more people pledged their lives to the King.

Chapter 2

~

T he King stood alone upon the high hill, dressed in a simple robe of homespun, and all the nations were arrayed in the fields below him. Heads of State directed their generals, who coordinated their infantry, artillery, and airmen into regiments, battalions, and squadrons. Magnates hired mercenaries, assassins, and saboteurs, who maneuvered themselves into strategic positions for attack. Civic groups organized themselves into militias and armed themselves with guns, knives, and clubs as they clustered together waiting for the fight to begin.

The Merchant stood off in the distance, watching.

"Once again, you have assembled against me, ready to raise arms in opposition to my reign," said the King as he looked out over the masses. "But please hear me, even now it is not too late.

"The first time you came against me in this way, I told you I loved you and could not bear to harm you. I allowed you to bring destruction upon me, because I wanted you to see that I will always hold your lives as more valuable than my own. I wanted to take your selfishness, your hatred, and your violence upon myself so you could leave it all behind and move forward and live a different life. Since my return, I have been offering you that life, a life of love and blessing, a life of joy and peace, a life with no need for selfishness, hatred, or violence. This is the life I offer you; won't you accept it?

"Many of your friends, neighbors, and fellow countrymen have accepted my offer, and they have been restored to me. They have been sharing in my work by helping those who are broken, lost, and in need, striving to establish goodness, equity, and justice in their communities, and delivering my words of guidance, encouragement, and correction to you. In response, you have slandered them, beaten them, and thrown them into prison. Your actions have exposed the futility of your ways and the misery they bring. And yet, even now, I offer you life; won't you accept it?

"The time has come to bring an end to the pain, division, and destruction you have inflicted upon yourselves and everyone across my Kingdom. If you reject the life I offer and insist on living for your own selfish desires, I will give you exactly what you demand: a life lived completely for yourself. You will spend the remainder of your years alone in the solitude of exile where you will no longer be able to inflict pain, conflict, and despair upon my Kingdom. But this need not be. You can still be restored to me, if only you will turn, receive my love, and embrace me for what I truly and rightfully am: your King and the King of everything. I offer this life to you one final time. Please, won't you accept it?"

Each of those who had assembled against the King stood silent with tears filling their eyes.

But then the voice of the Merchant echoed across the wide field. "Lies," he cried. "Lies most foul! He speaks of love, honor, and justice out of one side of his mouth, while, out of the other, he rants on and on about domination, enslavement, and repressing your every desire. What of the freedom you have fought so hard to win for yourselves? What of all you have accomplished for your own enjoyment? What of the well-earned dignity he would have you cast aside? And look at him! He stands alone and unarmed. How long will you be cowed by his empty threats? How long will you be idle as he humiliates you? This is your chance! Put an end to his lies once and for all!"

The people blinked, looking back and forth between the Merchant and the King. Then one of those who had ruled over a prosperous nation lifted his voice and shouted, "Freedom!" Instantly, everyone else joined him.

Orders were issued for the attack. Leaders, soldiers, and people of every sort rushed the hill, aiming their weapons at the King.

The King spread out his arms, and there appeared myriads upon myriads of fiery warriors brandishing swords and spears of living flame. Lightning flashed as they clashed their weapons and thunder boomed as they roared with fury. A terrible cry shook the air, and all saw the Merchant being shackled with burning chains and hauled off by a flock of the King's guard. Then the fearsome warriors fell upon all those who had assembled against the King, and every man and woman found themselves disarmed and bound with cords of light, and they were carried away with blinding speed to their exile.

In a moment, it was over.

Chapter 3

~

M itzi McDougal hugged her mother. Then, looking this way and that, she ran across the grass of the palace lawn. Stopping to catch her breath, she heard giggling from behind one of the trees in a nearby copse. She tiptoed around its trunk and found Fareed and Azim scuffling to stifle each other's mirth. They squealed with delight when they saw her, and, scrambling to their feet, they sprinted away as she gave chase.

"Go get them, Mitzi!" the King shouted as they bolted past him, and everyone laughed.

"I still haven't gotten used to it," Olivia Gonzalez said as she carried little Diego on her shoulders. "Letting our children play without fear."

"I know what you mean," Zoya Sokolov said, giving her Inessa's hand a squeeze. "It seems so unreal."

"And yet, here we are!" laughed Kemala Rahman.

"We are living the life that was always ours to have with you, my King," said her husband.

"Yes, Angga," the King said, patting the man on his shoulder. "My heart is bursting with joy!"

They walked along the path out of the park and into the palace gardens. They saw Song Xiao and Tomas Hernandez working together as they guided the oxen and plowed the ground.

"Hello, my friends!" the King called to them. "What will you be planting in this patch of earth?"

"We are in serious need of more melons!" Xiao called back.

"We have collected seeds for cantaloupe, honeydew, and watermelons," Tomas added. "They should do quite well in this soil."

"That sounds delightful!" the King said. "Thank you both for working so hard to provide us with such delicacies!"

∼

The company changed paths and climbed up the slope towards the palace. Once inside, they found a bustle of activity within the Great Hall.

Sitting around a giant woven rug near the hearth, several children listened to Anyango Mukondi as she read them a storybook. Okeyo stood by her side, acting out each scene with comic exaggeration, leaving the young ones rolling around with laughter. Anyango paused when she saw the King, and her eyes shone with gratitude as she reached over and gave Okeyo's arm a caress.

"Ah, there you are!" Rodrigo Torres said. He and Martina crossed the hall, each carrying a steaming bowl. Song Mei, Emem Omezi, and Annika Koslov followed along with their own dishes. "We have been doing some experimentation," Rodrigo continued, "and we wanted your opinion."

"Yes," said Mei. "We have been creating innovations on chicken soup with the vegetables and spices of our own homelands."

"To be honest," Emem laughed, "we are very proud of ourselves! We wanted to share the results with you."

"We brought enough spoons for everyone," Annika said, smiling.

One after another, the King and his party tasted each soup. They enjoyed the blends of chicken broth with the recipes: chili and lime mixed with tomatoes and onions; ginger and pepper sautéed with snow peas and bok choy; coriander and sesame stewed with okra and squash; garlic and vinegar simmered with beets and cabbage.

"They are all excellent!" declared the King, and the cooks congratulated each other.

~

"My King!" Safi Hakim hailed as he crossed the busy room. "I am so glad I found you! May our committee speak with you for a moment?"

"Of course, my friend," laughed the King, embracing the man when he came within reach. "Lead the way!"

Safi brought him down a short corridor off the Great Hall and into a side room. A handful of people sat together around a table covered by lists, maps, and blueprints.

"My King, as you know, we have been looking at the housing for your people," Safi said. "While everyone's basic needs are being met, we think we can make some improvements."

"What do you have in mind?" asked the King.

"Several things, actually," Amara Nnamdi said. "First of all, we would like to propose building several more tracks of homes over the eastern hills. Things have become a little too compact around here, and we would like to offer folks more room to breathe."

"Yes," Dayo Edozie said. "And it would be a simple matter to extend utilities to that area, and to build roads and paths to connect it with the other settlements around the palace."

"Plus," Amara added, "it is a beautiful spot with lovely views of both the mountains to the north and the ocean to the west. Whoever settles there will be richly blessed."

"That sounds very good," said the King. "What else?"

"Though we need to expand," Felipe Medina said, "we want to be careful not to lose our sense of connection together. We have been talking about creating more spaces for people to gather where they can enjoy each other's company."

"Yes," Gary Richards said, "and we thought that if we created a few more parks, a couple of extra community halls, some amphitheaters for public performances, along with coffee shops here and there, we could promote a regular rhythm to help people share their lives together."

"That is a very good idea," the King said. "Joy is the dish that feeds our life, and joy is always best when shared. I am excited to see how creative our people will be with putting these spaces to use!"

"Yes," Endora Samaras said, "but to make the most of these meeting places, people from across the region will need to be able to travel to them. This is why we have drawn up plans for expanding public transportation."

"We are thinking of adding a fleet of autobuses," Cynthia Hutchins said, pointing to a diagram resting on the table, "as well as four new tracks for the light rail."

"Yes, and bicycles," Safi said. "Lots and lots of bicycles."

The King laughed. "I love bicycles," he said, "and goodness knows our bodies can always use the exercise. You have all done great work here. Thank you for putting such care into honoring others and finding ways to improve their lives. We all will be blessed through your efforts! When the company of engineers finalize your plans, I will free up the guild of builders to begin making them a reality."

～

The King made his way to the throne room, where the delegates awaited him. He embraced each of the men and women before they took their seats. "I am so glad to see you all," he said. "I have been longing for this chance to look into your faces and to hear about developments across the Kingdom."

"Ah, it is such a joy to be with you, my King," Catalina Suarez said, "and I am so happy to be able to report great improvements. I feared we would never recover from the disastrous deforestation inflicted by the nations upon the lands to the south. But, after your visit, the ground became reinvigorated, and the saplings we planted have taken root and are growing at a surprising rate."

"I am glad," the King said, smiling. "Those had been such beautiful forests, and they provided us with so much fresh air to breathe. It is good to partner with them for the good of all."

"Yes," Irungu Kamau said, "and, with your guidance, we have been able to locate and dismantle caches of the nations' weaponry in the west. There is still much to be done to make the lands safe for resettlement, but we are making great progress. We are recycling all we find, and we will put the materials to use for the common good."

"Excellent," said the King. "The nations sought the power of destruction, but we will flourish through the power of restoration."

"We have been hard at work in the east," Li Jian said. "So many men, women, and children had been broken through the slavery and exploitation the nations inflicted upon them. Your healing their physical wounds, along with the love you poured out upon their hearts, has brought them out of the grip of despair, but it will take time for them to fully recover."

"Yes," said the King, "the human heart is a fragile thing; this kind of healing cannot be rushed. I will come again soon and help you continue this work."

"I am very sorry to say that my report is not as positive as the others, my King," Mrs. Merriweather said.

"What is it, Myrtle?"

"Despite all our best efforts, the lands in the north remain corrupted by the toxins the nations dumped into the air, water, and soil. We have not been able to purify things nearly enough. I'm afraid it remains a disaster area."

"That was my concern," the King said, shaking his head. "But do not give up hope. I am the King of everything, and my power and authority extend even to the pollutants that have infected my Kingdom. I will come and bring healing to the land."

"Thank you, my King," Mrs. Merriweather said. "You are such a dear."

~

After the evening's feast, people formed clusters for conversation, singing, and storytelling. The King went out to the westward balcony with two mugs of cocoa and sat down next to little Mishka. They silently sipped their drinks while they watched the sky turn from blue to orange and violet, and then to indigo as the last of the sun light was spent.

"How was your day?" the King asked the boy.

"Good," he said. "I helped with the chickens in the morning, and I played with Amir in the afternoon. I had a nice time."

"I am glad," the King said.

"How was your day," Mishka asked.

"Good," said the King. "I met with different people, and we worked on a number of things together. I dearly love each of them, and everything they are doing is truly good, so it was all a joy for me."

"I'm glad," Mishka said.

"There is a lot of work left to do," the King said, patting the boy on his shoulder. "Are you up for it?"

"If I can be with you, then I'm up for anything," Mishka said, patting the King on his arm.

"That is good," the King said. "And the nice thing is, we have all the time in the world and more to do it!"

Epilogue

~

O nce and for all time there is a King who is the King of everything. He is a good King, and he loves his people, and his people love him. Though they had once turned away from him, he sacrificed everything and restored his people to him. The King knows everyone in his Kingdom by name, and his greatest joy is to be with his people, and to share in their lives and bring them joy. And that is just what he is doing, and what he will continue to do forever and ever and evermore.